Medic

Bianca Lewis

Contents

Chapter 1. Touch Down

The plane touched down on the frost ridden runway and woke you from a restless sleep. The flight hadn't been an overly smooth one and despite the many hours you'd been in the air you'd had very little rest, your body ached for a comfortable bed.

Rubbing your tired eyes you rummaged around in your pack and glanced over your transfer papers, making sure to keep them to hand to give them to the commanding officer...whoever they were.

Your new base was situated off the beaten track in the arse end of nowhere, you'd been told very little about it, other than the nearest city was Kazan, the largest city of Tatarstan, Russia.You'd had a brief check on your phone to scope out the vibe of the general area, you might not have been told much but you wanted to at least get a feeling of the climate this time of year, at present it was -26 outside, a far cry from the blazing heat of your previous Iranian outpost.You quietly prayed that they'd have weather appropriate gear to give you, because other than your 20kilo pack of desert-ready clothing, you had fuck all.

The moment the aircraft door opened you felt the air being knocked straight out of you, the sheer intensity of the cold here was unlike anything you'd every experienced before. Bundling your collar shut in a meagre attempt to keep your neck warm you quickly exited the plane and were met by a new face. Before all else, the first thing you noticed about this man was his distinctive mohawk, you'd been told that this base was unlike any other that you'd been stationed at before but you'd assumed that was simply to do with the environment...not the complete lack of standard military dress code.

"Oi oi, took ya long enough! Welcome to paradise!"

That was the second thing you noticed, his thick Scottish accent. Despite his loud and rather over-the-top first impression the man had an extremely warm and welcoming aura about him, almost goofy. You knew you'd get on well with him.

"Sergeant John MacTavish, call me Soap, nice to meet you, doctor."

He grabbed your hand and gave it a firm shake before you even have time to register that he offered you a hand to shake in the first place. You grinned at his odd callsign and made a mental note to yourself to ask him how he got it later on.

"P-pleased to meet you, Soap. Please just call me Dove, there's no need for formalities."

The Scottish soldier grinned, idly rubbing the thin scar that ran down one eyebrow and onto his cheekbone.

"Right you are, Dove! Come on then follow me, freezin' my tits off out 'ere."

Again before you had time to respond, Soap had turned on his heel and was quickly marching himself in the direction of the nearest building on the base. You quickly slung your pack over your shoulder and offered the pilot a nod in thanks for the smooth flight over before you jogged after him, eager to not miss out on anything Sergeant MacTavish had to tell you about what to expect from life on your new base.

"First stop is handing the boss your papers, then I'll take ya to your new digs n' let you settle in." Soap grinned at you from over his shoulder, his quick pace a testament to the excitement of having someone new to give the grand tour of the base to.

"The boss?" You had to raise your voice slightly to compensate the wind that was beginning to whistle between the walls of the base, the sheer ferocity of the cold bit into your cheeks and ears as you felt them burning in futility to keep you warm. Soap spun to face you, opting to walk backwards for a spell as he addressed the obvious confusion in your voice.

"Damn you've really not been told anythin' about us have you? Eh, probably for the best. Captain Price is who we're off to see, you'll like him. Kinda like our base dad, though don't go tellin' him I told you that."

The Sergeant gave you another playful grin and turned back around to face the correct way. You couldn't help but chuckle, despite how tired you were from the flight you couldn't wait to meet the rest of your new team mates and you wondered silently if they'd be as...quirky, as Soap.

It wouldn't be long until you found out just how quirky your new team was.

Chapter 2. Take A Seat

E dited 21/05/23 - clearer read, spelling and grammar changes, fleshed bits out.

-

"Dove, it's a pleasure to meet you, I've heard some good things about you."

Captain Price leaned over his desk and firmly shook your hand. You gave the superior officer a polite smile and handed him your transfer papers before taking a seat opposite him from behind a splintering old table. A cup of what looked to be piping hot coffee puffed steam between the two of you and a small part of you wished you could wrap your hands around the mug. Despite only being outside for a few minutes at most your fingers were chilled to the bone.

"It's a pleasure to meet you, Captain. I'm excited to be a part of the 141, though I hope I won't be needed too much."

Price shot you a crooked smile and huffed in mild amusement, idly scratching the back of his neck.

"You'll be seeing a lot of them, I'm sure. They find a way of getting into shit one way or another, so don't go easy on them. You're chief medical officer here, not their nanny."

Price took a small sip of his coffee before humming mid drink as though he'd just remembered something, his eyes narrowing slightly as he rushed to swallow down his drink before addressing you again.

"Ah, also, you won't just be taking care of our 141 lads, you've also got KorTac to deal with."

You raised an eyebrow quizzically, "KorTac, sir?"

Soap, seeing that his captain was again mid-drink through his coffee, pushed himself off of the doorframe he was leant on and filled you in on the situation. The expression of total confusion obviously that evident on your face that you didn't even need to ask for the information before it was offered to you freely by the Scotsman.

"KorTac are an independent military contractor outfit, doc."

"Military contractors?" You we're still confused.

"They'll do dirty work for the highest paying military outfit. Pretty much military mercenaries..." Soaps tone was questionable and gave you the impression that these KorTac people weren't the most popular on the campus.

"They're a bit more than that, Sergeant." Price leaned back into his chair, the metal joints creaking slightly as it balanced on two legs whilst support-ing the officers weight.

"A little over two months back we were force-merged with KorTac as a last ditch attempt to avoid conflict while based here. They're a band of international special forces agents for hire that various governments use to conduct various operations globally."

"Aye." Soap interjected. "Currently the KorTac operatives are staying with us until we've finished what we need to here, how long that'll be is anyones guess. They aren't all bad, but obviously the 141 are way better, isn't that right, sir?" Soap gave you a wink and leaned against the wall closest to you, giving his Captain a cheeky grin and earning a withering look from his superior officer in return.

"I think what Soap is trying to say, is that while we're all under one roof you'll be expected to act as the doctor to all of us." Price's gaze flicked to Soap, giving him a nod towards the door, the Scottish soldier needed no further instruction and headed back out of the office.

For a few moments the Captain simply studied you, running a calloused hand through his thick mutton chop-styled beard.

"Soap'll see you to your infirmary, everything you need is already ready and waiting. Once you're settled feel free to make yourself acquainted with all of the troops, we've some pretty interesting characters here as I'm sure you'll soon find out if you haven't already. Good luck with them, and welcome to the team."

You shook Price's hand once again before giving a polite nod and turning to leave his office. Instantly you spotted Sergeant MacTavish. Soap had been patiently waiting for you and seemed eager to show you to your new digs.

□ □ MEDIC □ □

It had been a few hours since Soap had given you a tour of the base and shown you to your new room and infirmary. You'd quickly unpacked what little supplies you had brought with you and were now focused on making yourself acquainted with each soldiers medical records. To say they were inconsistent was an understatement...

While some of the soldiers records were pages long, listing everything from minor paper cuts to broken bones, others were almost completely blank, giving just the most basic information such as the operatives callsign and place of origin.

You leaned back in your desk chair and gave a heavy sigh, rapidly clicking through the myriad of records still yet to be properly filled in. There was no real way of getting these missing details filled in quickly and requesting a file transfer from the higher ups would potentially take weeks, if not longer.

You figured the quickest way to get up to date was to call up the missing personnel one at a time and perform a quick medical on each of them, if anything you'd be killing two birds with one stone by introducing yourself to some of the operatives whilst learning what you needed to. It was perfect.

You grabbed the intercom microphone that was sat on your desk side and tapped it idly, pausing for a moment to think about what you'd say before you pressed the button to speak. You could hear the echo of your own voice through the base as you made your announcement, it always made you cringe a little inside.

"Attention please, this is Dove, your new medical officer. Can the soldiers with the following call-signs please report to the infirmary for medical evaluation: Ghost, Roach, Horangi and König. Again, that's Ghost, Roach, Horangi and König to the infirmary, thank you."

You slumped back into your seat, breathing out a heavy sigh and wondering why you felt so nervous. You'd done that hundreds of times before and that one shouldn't have been any different. Perhaps it was due to the fact that you'd never met these soldiers before and weren't sure what to expect. Either way, despite your nerves you were excited to become acquainted with more of your team and you eagerly awaited their arrival to the infirmary.

Roach was the first to arrive, a young soldier in his late twenties at best. From the offset he seemed eager to meet you and in many ways held similar vibes as Soap did upon your first dealings with him.

You explained the situation with his medical records and he was more than happy to fill in any and all blanks that you needed in order to complete his file. It wasn't long after that he gave a polite goodbye and left your station, leaving the next person to arrive almost immediately after.

Horangi made you laugh, he'd obviously just come in from the outside and was quite vocal in how much he hated the cold. The man was charming, seemingly intent on learning more about you rather than taking interest in what it was that you wanted with him to the point that you actually had to politely remind him of the reasons for calling him to your office in the first place.

Like Roach, Horangi was relatively open about filling in the blanks, though thankfully he had a relatively clean medical record, you figured he must be either exceptionally careful out in the field or have an occupation within the base that required him to operate at safe distance from the heavy action. Before leaving he made sure to tell you what time dinner and breakfast was so you wouldn't miss out. You'd already known the timetable for the general base operations, but it was extremely sweet nonetheless.

Next up was Ghost. You'd briefly laid eyes upon him in passing when you first got off the plane and was greeted by Soap, but he had kept his distance. It was only when he sauntered into your office that you managed to get a good look at him. To say the man was intimidating would have been an understatement.

Like Horangi, he had just come out from the cold and was wearing a distinct mask in the shape of a skull, you could see little of his face save for two exceptionally bored looking hazel eyes and contrasting blonde eyelashes which still had frost clinging to them from the extreme cold of the outside.

He said very little, simply asking what you wanted and you were quick to reply. It was evident that at this moment in time he had very little patience nor any desire to converse in any real detail other than what was required of him. Certainly a stark contrast to your last two patients who had come to visit you and seemingly welcomed you with open arms.

You rushed through the process as best you could, not wanting to waste his time and, quite frankly, feeling pretty intimidated by the large British man. Thankfully you got the majority of what you needed to in order to send him on his way.

You slumped back into your chair, pushing yourself back and forth idly on its wheels before glancing at your checklist. Only one soldier remained, König.

You sat patiently and waited, watching the clock for a spell before going back to your paperwork and making sure everything had been filled in correctly. Periodically you glanced at the clock, noticing it was getting later and later each time you looked at it.

Eventually it got to the point where you'd resigned yourself to the fact that this König, whoever they were, wasn't coming and you decided it was best to shut up shop for the evening and have an early night. Hours on end of flying had worked up a sizeable knot in your back muscles and you were eager to test out your new mattress, hoping it would be softer than the one in your last station.

You'd find out who the mystery soldier was soon enough and grab what details you needed from them to finish your files. For now it was time to rest up and recover from your jet lag.

Chapter 3. An Awkward Encounter

Edited 21/05/23 - fleshed chapter out more. Spelling and grammar changes.

-

The following morning you awoke feeling relatively refreshed and eager to start your day.

You'd had a deep, dreamless sleep, too exhausted from your transfer the previous day for your brain to formulate any far fetched imagery through the night. You'd always had vivid dreams, dreams that felt real, you'd be able to smell, feel, taste. Every night your head would take you to a far away place, one night you could be slaying dragons and driving super cars way above your pay grade, other nights were a little more close to home, saving soldiers whose injures were so grievous you could swear you could smell the iron in their blood as it poured out onto your table.

You didn't care much for those kinds of dreams, you always ended up losing the poor soul you were tasked with saving.

You quickly got dressed and brushed your teeth. From the moment you opened your eyes you were acutely aware of the goal you'd set yourself for the day and that was to complete the last missing medical record of the mystery soldier "König".

Despite your tannoy announcement they were the only one who didn't show up at your office and rather than assuming they ignored you completely you opted to believe the soldier was either busy at the time of your announcement or simply not in the base all together. That was what you hoped was the case at-least.

By the time you'd gotten to the mess hall the majority of the soldiers had finished their breakfast and had gone about their business. Thankfully you'd spotted a couple of familiar faces sitting at the far side table.

Soap was the first to notice you, giving you an enthusiastic wave and gesturing for you to come and join them for breakfast, you were more than happy to oblige.

"Mornin', doc. Good sleep?" Soaps tone was nothing but bright as he picked at the scrambled eggs on his plate.

You gave a smile and a nod, cupping a glass of fresh orange juice between both of your hands, "Good morning, Soap. As a matter of fact I've not gotten to sleep so quickly in...psh I don't know how long."

Horangi, one of the soldiers you had brought in for a medical the day before, sat to the side of you, his keen hazel eyes studying you.

"You gather the rest of your intel?"

You shot the Korean operative a puzzled look and he grinned in response.

"Your files? Missing medical records? What, you forgot about them already?"

You rolled your eyes, smirking at him and feeling thankful that there were at least a couple soldiers on this base so far that you felt comfortable to have a joke with. You stared into your cup of juice and swilled it around a little, eyeing up your blurred reflection in the surface of the glass.

"I'll have you know, Horangi, that my acquisition of the intel was a succe ss...for the most part anyway."

"Oh?" Soap perked up, his interest obviously piqued.

"I'm missing one last record off the list, then you're all up to date in my files." You confirmed.

"Fifty quid says it's König you're missing?"

You paused briefly and eyed Soap, half suspicious and half impressed at his correct assumption.

"How'd you know?"

"Because the guy didn't show up for any medicals with our previous doctor either. Hell I'm not even sure he met the last doctor and that was despite two months of living on the same base as each other before the poor bastard got K.I.A."

"Oh. He's out in the field a lot then, this König?" You ask simply, earning a snort from Horangi who was now idly pushing toast crumbs around his plate.

"He's out there no more than the rest of us. It's just the way he is. König is...eh, a bit of a mystery. I've worked with him in KorTac for just over two years now and I still barely know shit about him.."

Horangi noticed the concern on your face and gave you a gentle nudge with his elbow.

"Don't get me wrong, he's a nice guy once he opens up a little...its just getting to that part that's difficult."

You placed your cup down with a heavy thud against the table, resting your head against one of your hands. "Well that's ridiculous! Surely someone knows something about him! Mystery or not, I need to update his files, as this bases only doctor right now I need as much information on each soldier as possible. Like it or not he's coming to see me today."

You notice Soap and Horangi exchange glances with one another and then back to you, it was as if they'd just made a silent bet with one another on if you'd actually acquire Königs updated records by the end of the day.

You huffed under your breath, crossing your arms. "At this rate I'm going to have to ask Captain Price to pull rank and force him to my infirmary..."

"Or you can just ask König to come see you for his medical yourself." Soap replied simply.

You shoot him an 'I would if I could' look and raised an eyebrow in confusion when he gave a brief nod of his head to gesture behind you, urging you to turn to look over your shoulder. That was the first moment you laid eyes on your mystery soldier who had just walked into the mess hall.

You immediately excused yourself and approached König. It wasn't until you got up close to him that you realised just how fucking enormous he was. The man literally towered above you and his face was completely obscured by a sniper hood save for two glacial grey eyes that reminded you of the harsh climate outside of your bases walls.

"König?"

You tried your best to sound polite and professional though it was pretty damn hard when you were having to almost strain your neck to look directly at the man.

"Ja? Can I help you?" König replied, his tone even.

"You can actually..." you smiled briefly before continuing.

"I'm Dove, your new medical officer, I noticed yesterday you didn't come for your medical?" You noticed the mountain of a man tense slightly as he shifted his weight from one leg to the other.

"Ah."

You waited a couple seconds, hoping there would be more to that response than just ah. There wasn't. You cleared your throat, trying to put on a more stern and professional tone.

"Ahem w-well it's important that we get this medical done, König. You're the only one left with missing details that I need to update."

"Not necessary. I am in fine health." He replied simply and turned around to leave the mess hall, despite not grabbing any breakfast he was evidently done being in your presence.

Without thinking you grabbed the sleeve of his shirt, he halted immediately, his head snapping back to meet your gaze.

Due to the hood you couldn't get an accurate read on Königs expression and this only served to make you more nervous. You were pretty sure this man could literally snap you in two across his knee like a twig. Thankfully Horangi, God bless him, had noticed you were struggling and sauntered over to the rescue.

"Oi, König, you really gonna disappoint our new doctor?" Horangi grinned, elbowing his enormous team mate playfully.

Königs grey eyes flicked between you and the other soldier, his fingers tapping against the side of his thigh as he seemed to consider what Horangi had said to him before releasing a long sigh which made his hood puff out slightly.

"Fine."

Immediately your eyes lit up and you turned to Horangi who gave you a charismatic grin. At this point König had already begun, rather dejectedly, walking in the direction of the infirmary.

"I'd catch up to him if I were you, before he runs off."

Horangi gave you a playful elbow in your side, you smirked back at him, whispering a quick thank you before rushing out of the mess hall to catch up with König. With legs as long as his, it was a bigger challenge than you expected.

Chapter 4. Name and Date of Birth?

Edited 21/05/23 - grammar and spelling revamp. Slight flesh out of text.

-

Despite König leaving for the infirmary only moments before you, you almost had to break into a sprint to catch up with him. Just one of his normal strides was equal to two, perhaps even three of your own. The man was insanely tall so you supposed it made sense but even still....

"Thank you for agreeing to help fill in these missing records, König." You gave him a warm smile and glanced up at him.

His cold grey eyes briefly flicked down to you and then back up ahead. "I did not have much say in the matter."

"No, I suppose you didn't. But thank you anyway." You laugh lightly, trying to ignore the rising tension that was accumulating in the pit of your stomach.

Before long you both got settled into the infirmary, you sat at your desk and logged in to find the files you needed to update. When you did find them you signaled for König to join you at your desk and look at your computer.

" See all these blanks? I need details for each one." You tapped the computer screen, pointing at each blank box in the soldiers files.

"Why." König responded. It wasn't a question, more of a statement.

"Well because if you ever get hurt out in the field I need to know your history so I can help you better." You replied with a smile.

König regarded you almost suspiciously for a moment and stared back at the computer screen. "Hm..."

You gesture to the chair opposite you and wait for him to sit, eventually he does, but the small desk chair seemed to groan under his weight.

"Ok so let's start from the top. You've more blanks on your file than Ghost and that's saying something. Name?"

"König."

"No, your actual name?"

"I don't see how this helps you look after me better." The soldier replied coldly.

You cleared your throat, the weight of Königs stare threatening to sink you into the ground."Yeah I guess I can't fault that logic. I'll just put your call sign in for now...says here you're 32, is that correct?"

"Ja.""Born in Salzburg, Austria?""Mhm""Any allergies to medicine or food?""Nein." "Aaaand your blood type is AB Positive?""Yup."

You confirmed the details that König gave you and pushed yourself away from your desk, walking over to the nearest medical gurney. You could feel

Königs eyes studying your every move in an almost predatory way which sent a shiver down your spine.You shot him a reassuring smile as you lay out a couple of supplies, ignoring the unfamiliar feeling of being scared by your own team mates presence.

"I doubt you're going to give me any more information even if I say pretty please, so let's move onto the physical." You stated with a warm smile.

Instantly you saw Königs entire body tense up, his gloved hands clasping together in unease as you turned and gestured for him to hop up onto the bed. He didn't move an inch, simply continuing to stare at you. You gestured again to the bed and raised an eyebrow.

"König?...Come on, the sooner you do this the sooner you can leave."

With a heavy sigh you watched the enormous soldier haul himself out of the chair and over to the bed, his icy grey eyes seemed to look through you, unfocused, uninterested, cold.

You grabbed your stethoscope from the table by your side and hooked it into your ears, noticing in your peripheral vision how Königs shoulders were tensed in anticipation. Despite his awkward and rather unapproachable demeanour you honestly felt sorry for the guy. It didn't take a doctor to see his anxiety was through the roof. König didn't want to be anywhere near your proximity, you'd already been told by Soap and Horangi that he hated doctors to the extent of not even meeting the previous medic on site.

Pushing the overall awkwardness of the situation aside, you got back into your professional headspace and laid the stethoscope against Königs chest. His pectoral muscles twitched slightly at your touch and his eyes glanced at you briefly before shifting to one side. Honestly you couldn't help but silently admire the sheer amount of work that this man must have put in to get the physique that he had, under that black shirt he was absolutely solid.

"You've a strong heartbeat, very strong in fact." You smiled gently as you briefly caught Königs gaze. "Not a beat out of place, let's move on, shall we?"

You withdrew the stethoscope from Königs chest and couldn't help but smile when he released a small gasp of air, you realised he'd been holding his breath the entire time you'd been listening to his heartbeat.

"Next up is your blood pressure, ok?"

At this point you may have well been speaking to yourself, König was pretty much unresponsive to your attempts at conversation. You slipped the inflatable cuff over his hand and worked it up his bicep, struggling to get it where it needed to be from the sheer size of your patient. You'd had a similar experience trying to take Ghosts blood pressure the other day, it seemed the majority of the men on the base were stacked and, despite it impeding some of your medical processes, you found it very amusing that your standard equipment didn't seem to be designed for such a hunky group of fellas.

"Blood pressure is all good too, so far you're a picture of perfect health!" The air hissed out from the pressure cuff quickly, unable to maintain its shape around Königs huge arm. König wiggled his fingers slightly, allowing the circulation to come back into his digits properly before clamping his hands together and bringing them to rest on his thighs.

You put your equipment back away swiftly and sat back down at the desk to log the information you gathered throughout Königs physical examination, clasping your hands together with a loud slap upon completion.

"Ok, I think we're as up to date as we can be right now on your physical, there's just a few blanks on your psychiatric evaluation left to fill ou-"

Finally you looked back up from your computer, a very confused frown creasing your forehead as you scanned the infirmary.

König was no where to be seen, managing to slip out of your office while you were busy filling in the last of his credentials...for a man that big you honestly didn't think it would be possible.

Yet here you were, alone.

Chapter 5. Snowfall

E dited 21/05/23 - minor changes to grammar & spelling.

The month that followed your transfer had been blissfully uneventful, as boring as sitting around checking emails was it was always somewhat of a relief knowing that none of the soldiers in your care actually needed you.

Ghost had come to visit a few times for a top up on some tablets to help with insomnia, you'd suggested he take them during his initial medical to try and help him get a little more sleep and judging by the fact he was wanting more it seemed to be working for him, for now at least.

Soap and Horangi were also regular visitors at your infirmary, though their visits were purely for recreational purposes, you enjoyed their company and they two always seemed to brighten up your day and make you laugh with their rather crude humour. Since KorTac and the 141 had merged both Soap and his Korean counterpart had seemed to get quite close, of course the relationship that Soap seemed to share with Lieutenant Ghost was second to none, but Horangi seemed to enjoy winding people up just as much as the Scot did, so they became partners in crime more often than not.

Today you'd finished up what little work you had much earlier than you anticipated and decided to head out for a walk around the grounds of the base. Despite the cripplingly cold weather Russia had to offer you'd barely ventured out around the area and felt it was way overdue.

You bundled yourself up as best as you could, wearing as many layers as your coat would allow and still be able to zip up. Temperatures in Kazan regularly dropped to -26 degrees Celsius, coupled with the wind chill factor it didn't make going outside a particularly enjoyable experience for anyone, even for the soldiers in the base that had originated from equally cold climates.

Today, however, the weather seemed a little more forgiving and you were greeted by gently falling puffs of snow. For a while you simply looked out over the vast landscape and hugged yourself, allowing yourself to feel each individual snowflake that kissed your skin, the blanket of fluff deadened sound from miles around, leaving you stood surrounded by a silence that you'd not experienced for years.

Suddenly you were brought out of your daydreaming when you caught sight of a figure in your peripheral vision, around a hundred feet away from you stood König, you'd not seen the huge soldier at all since your rather awkward medical with him, even when you joined the group for breakfast and tea in the mess hall you'd not seen him once. For such a large guy he seemed to know exactly how to keep himself hidden, especially from you and in the back of your mind you could hear Horangi's voice reminding you just how much König hated doctors.

Against your better judgement you decided to approach the Austrian, you'd said to Soap when you first arrived that you wanted to be friends with as many of the troops as possible, now was your shot to add another name to your mentally logged friends list.

The crunch of the snow under your feet had König alerted to you well before you managed to get close to him, for a moment you genuinely thought he would turn and walk away from you before you managed to trudge through the snow to meet him. Thankfully he didn't, though he did eye you somewhat sceptically when you finally reached him.

"Good afternoon, König! Have you come out here to enjoy the snow too?" You gave him your warmest smile as you craned your neck to actually look him in the eyes. Like the last time, his eyes were the only thing you could properly see due to his sniper hood covering the rest of his face.

König regarded you silently for a moment, his breath visible in a small icy cloud of vapour as he gave a slight huff."Ah...Yes, I suppose." He tilted his head slightly, focusing on a particularly large snowflake that drifted by the two of you.

"Do you get snow like this back home?" You asked warmly, in the back of your mind you were desperately clutching at straws to keep the conversation going, even if it was a little while.

"Sometimes." He replied simply.

"When was the last time you went home?""Not for a very long time.""I guess KorTac don't get home leave the same way the military do, huh?"

König raised an eyebrow from behind his hood and breathed out a heavy sigh before turning and walking in the opposite direction, you were quick to follow behind him.

The large soldier briefly glanced over his shoulder, noticing that you were still following him, stopping dead in his tracks so suddenly that you walked straight into the back of him. Your attention had been focused more on the snow and ice under your feet rather than what König was doing in front of you.

König turned back around to face you, while you couldn't see his face you knew for a fact he had an exasperated expression purely from the way he simply stood and regarded you.Truthfully? You knew you were being annoying, though you'd prefer to call it "persistent". This man intrigued you, you wanted to learn more about him, just as you did with Soap, Horangi and the other men under your care.

"Doctor..." König's voice was straining to remain polite at this point, though he continued to remain courteous."Is there any reason why you are following me?"

You swallowed the lump of anxiety building in your throat and shot the soldier a crooked smile, gesturing to the snow as you did so.

"Well I didn't expect anyone else to be out here, to be honest. When I saw you I figured I may as well enjoy the snow with someone else rather than on my own. Besides, I've not seen you at all since you ducked out on me during your medical. Never even had the chance to do routine blood work."

König seemed to tense up, obviously hoping that you'd forgotten that he slipped out during the back end of his examination with you. You watched in silent amusement as the man shuffled awkwardly in the snow, squeezing the back of his neck as he tried to look anywhere else but at you.

"Ah... Das tut mir leid- sorry about that, I...I do not like doctors very much." König's accent seemed a little thicker as he floundered to justify himself, you couldn't help but smile gently.

"You don't have to like doctors, König. Let's face it, no one likes doctors, but maybe you could learn to like me? The other guys have." You considered the possibility of giving the enormous soldier a friendly slap on the arm but faltered, opting to swing your arms back and forth awkwardly.

"I'm not sure that came out the way you'd intended for it to, doctor." König stated dryly, the brief glimpse of a raised eyebrow from under his hood showing confused annoyance.

Your eyes widened in realisation of how that must have sounded and immediately you ran a hand through your hair.

"I-I didn't mean it like that at all! What I meant was tha-"Before you had chance to finish justifying yourself, König once again turned and walked in your opposite direction, leaving you flustered and alone as the snow began to get heavier.

This time you didn't follow him.

Chapter 6. Make The Effort

E dited 21/05/23 - minor changes to format and spelling.

-

"Come on, König! Give em a chance!"

Soap buckled himself into his seat in the chopper, making sure the straps were adjusted properly and securely. Orders had come in from on high for a small selection of the KorTac and 141 troops to head out on a recon mission a hundred clicks or so North of the base, rumours were spreading that an infamous Russian drug lord was holed up in the area and was exchanging his wears for imported United States weaponry. The US wanted to know just who was supplying these weapons at the source, that was providing the rumours and intel were true.

Price had been assured the mission would be relatively risk free, the team was to go and purely scout out for general intel, to try build a better picture of what exactly was going on and if it was even worth further action. König knew better than to trust the words of some high-up military fat cat who'd probably not seen a day of conflict in his life. Something would go wrong, something always went wrong. Call it pessimistic, but it was that over cautious pessimism that had kept König alive so far.

König huffed in mild annoyance at Soaps pestering, rolling his sniper hood up over his head and placing it on his lap. While it certainly wasn't a common occurrence to see the huge Austrian soldier without his trademark face covering, he didn't live inside of it in quite the same way as Ghost did.

"Sergeant, I do not need to make friends with the new doctor." König growled lightly, reaching into his pocket for his packet of cigarettes, he lit the end, taking a needlessly large drag to steady his nerves.

"Sure ya do!" the Scotsman grinned.

"Why exactly are you so insistent on this, Soap?"

"Because Dove is trying to be friends with all of us, least you could do is make a little effort, ye great big awkward bastard." Soap elbowed his team mate playfully, attempting to lighten the situation.

König rolled his eyes, leaning over and resting his head in a gloved hand.

"I am not fond of Doctors." König stated, idly scratching at his stubble whilst Soap batted away some wayward smoke.

"You keep smoking those things and you'll be seeing a lot more of the good doctor than just for a routine checkup." Soap feigned a cough, sticking his tongue out. König stifled a quiet laugh, crushing out his cigarette onto the underside of his boot before flicking it out of the chopper doors before they shut.

The large soldier leaned back in his seat, his leg bouncing idly as he allowed his mind to wander. He thought about what the Sergeant had said, about at-least trying to make some semblance of effort with the new doctor.

König hadn't even known what the previous medic had looked like until he saw the man's lifeless body being wheeled into the base after being KIA.

König had met this new medic within the first day or so of them touching down and, granted, they did seem to be trying their darnedest at befriending everyone on the base. Thinking back to his previous conversations with the doctor, König couldn't help but feel the slightest twinge of guilt at being so distant with Dove.

It wasn't that König was an unfriendly person or considered the doctor beneath his station to talk to, not at all. The simple fact of the matter was that the Austrian simply sucked ass at talking to people in general, especially people who he'd just met and especially doctors whose only purpose was to poke, prod and cause you pain.

When König was recruited to KorTac it had taken months for him and Horangi to have a steady conversation and banter with one another, and even now after working together for the better part of two years the Korean soldier actually knew scarily little about his much larger team mate.

In the case of Soaps relationship with the Austrian it was simply that from the moment they were introduced the Scotsman had followed König around, pestering him at every given opportunity, making sure he was party to every event on the base. The huge soldier had very little say in the matter, Soap wanted them to be friends with him and so König had to come to terms with that fact and tolerate him, though he'd have been lying if he said that Soap wasn't enjoyable to be around.

"Dove is actually pretty sweet, chingu."

Horangi shouted over the drone of the helo's propellers. Soap grinned as he watched König run a gloved hand over his face in mild annoyance.

"Verdammt noch mal, you're ganging up on me too, Horangi? I thought we were team mates."

The Korean soldier laughed loudly, picking up on the slight hint of amusement in Königs voice despite his otherwise jaded expression.

"Sorry, chingu! But MacTavish is right for once. Stop being such an anti-social asshole."

"I second that!" Roach shouted up, opting to finally pitch in on the conversation.

"Alright! Mein Gott of all the team mates to be stuck with on this missio n..."

□ □ MEDIC □ □

You sat back in your desk chair, it's old fixings groaning slightly as you leaned back as far as the chair would allow. Idly you looked through the list of operatives that had been sent out on a recon mission some three days before.

Soap, Horangi, Roach, König, Runner, Bolt.

The last two call signs you weren't familiar with and you had to bring up their individual files to scan through the details. The two of them were fresh blood to 141, having being transferred together at the same time around a week before you arrived. Both men had full medical records, so it made sense you'd not met them as it was only the soldiers with lacking information that you'd really had a proper talk to.

Roach, despite a complete file, had spent almost the same amount of time in your office as Soap and Horangi, eager to come and meet his new medic. He was a sweet guy and you'd taken to calling him your "little bug" whenever he'd pass you in the hallway. The man seemed to enjoy the spin you'd put on his callsign.

"Look alive, Doc. We've got casualties incoming, ETA seven minutes."

Captain Price's gravelly voice echoed over the tannoy in your infirmary and instantly your stomach dropped. You stood rapidly, your desk chair wheeling itself away from you as you rushed to prep the med bay. The ever increasing drone of an incoming helicopter made you acutely aware that it wouldn't be long before you had to get to work and potentially save these men.

No sooner had you set up your station a group of soldiers came rushing in carrying two bodies. The first one, you noted, was already dead. The young man's carotid artery had been torn completely open on one side of his neck, most likely from a bullet.

The second man was covered in what appeared to be severe burns, his tactical gear had melted to his skin in some areas. You'd never get used to that smell. Instantly you got to work, shooing the soldiers away that had brought the men in and proceeding to hook the still living man up to various wires and tubes. Not much was certain, but you did know that if this soldier survived, his life wouldn't ever be the same.

You'd worked for what felt like hours to stabilise the soldier, having to intubate him and bring him back from the brink several times before his body seemed to settle and accept the drugs you were feeding him. The man was in an induced coma, it was the only way you saw fit to make sure you could work without fear of him waking, though given the nature of his injuries it would have been highly unlikely.

With a heavy sigh you slumped back into your chair, allowing yourself a brief moment of rest. Right now there was little more to be done other than wait and see if the man would continue to remain stable. A soft knock on the door broke you away from your thoughts and you glanced up, relieved to see Soap. To say the man looked tired would have been an understatement, dark rings clung to the Scotsman's eyes and he was sporting a rather large gash along the side of his head which he seemed to have patched up himself before coming to you.

"Soap...Jesus what happened out there?" Your voice was quiet and gentle as you gestured for the Sergeant to sit on a free bed and allow you to take a look at his injury. He did so with no complaint.

"Things didn't go according to plan." Soap huffed, his eyes flicking over to the white bodybag that you'd put the other dead soldier in. You shone a light into the wound on the sergeants head, pleased to see that he'd given it a thorough clean up. Other than a few butterfly stitches and a strong bottle of painkillers there was little left to do to help him.

"Are the others ok?" You ask quietly as you got to work putting some small adhesive strips over the top of Soaps wound. "As good as can be expected." "Horangi alright?""Few scrapes n' bumps, nothing major." Soap shrugged, wincing slightly at your touch. "Roach and König?" Soap smiled, giving you a reassuring slap on the side of your arm. "Roach doesn't have a mark on him. Königs...well, König. He got off the heli lookin' a little stiff, but I'm sure he's fine, he's not said anythin' to suggest otherwise."

You frowned a little at the sergeants response, granted you were very thankful that the majority of the team were back in one piece, but you weren't entirely convinced that everyone had gotten away lightly. Except for the two poor souls in your infirmary, of course.

"Can you bring König here for me please, Soap." You placed the last steri-strip over the Scot's injury and handed him a small packet of pain killers, no doubt the man would have a killer headache in the morning if he didn't already.

Soap glanced down at the painkillers, immediately popping two in his mouth and swallowing them dry, "Doc, the chances of König letting you check him over are slim to none, he seemed fi-"

"I'm not convinced." You interrupted, your voice remaining gentle but stern.

"Bring him to me, make him aware that it's not a request. It's a command from his medical officer."

Soap grinned, giving you a faux salute as he hopped off of the bed, briefly eyeing up your handiwork in the mirror.

"Aye aye, captain."

Chapter 7. Easy Does It

Edited 21/05/23 - spelling and grammar corrections. Small re-writes to flesh out dialogue.

-

It was around 40 minutes later when Soap came back. You were beginning to think he'd either forgotten due to the injury to his head, or König had outright refused to come see you despite making it a direct order, so you were oddly relieved when the colossal form of the Austrian ducked under the doorframe with Soap stood in front of him giving a cheeky grin.

"Looky who I've brought!" Soap puffed himself up a little in victory as he turned to look up at the huge soldier, giving him a solid clap on the back. You notice how Königs eyes briefly squeezed shut in a wince.

"You play nice and let the doctor do their thing, right, König? Good luck, Dove!" With a final chuckle the sergeant left the infirmary, leaving the two of you to stare at one another in awkward silence.

You smiled warmly at the huge Austrian stood in the doorway. König was wearing a tight fitting long sleeved black shirt and his usual cargo pants, his face is still covered by the sniper hood he always seems to wear around you.

"Welcome, König. I'm so pleased to see you back home safe." Your voice was gentle, warming. Inwardly you'd hoped he didn't begrudge you for having Soap wrangle him into the infirmary.

König didn't reply, opting to remain silent and tapped each of his fingers to his thumbs anxiously as he stood in the doorway. You signalled for him to take a seat and watched as he did so, albeit very stiffly despite his attempts at acting casual. Once sat down you spent a couple of moments opening Königs files, noticing from your peripheral vision how his leg bounced nervously and his eyes remained fixed on the tiled roof. This man was honestly a mystery. How could someone described as being such a weapon of mass destruction out on the field now be a seemingly nervous wreck?

You took a seat and took the time to visually assess him while you sterilised your hands and put your examination gloves on. Despite wearing a black shirt you could make out a darker wet patch on his side which was shining slightly in the overhead light. It was blood and you knew it. You could smell the copper it held in the air, you'd never forget that smell.

"So! How'd the mission go?"

"...Classified."

You scoff lightly "well yeah I know that, I don't need to know the ins and outs, but was it a success? Did you get done what you needed to? I hope so, given the cost..." your eyes flicked briefly to the body bag in the corner of the room and then over to the critically ill soldier who you'd previously stabilised.

König wrung his hands together and breathed out a shaky sigh,"Doctor... Respectfully, why am I here?" His tone was outwardly polite but evidently guarded.

You gave the soldier a warm smile, "I was tasked to make sure you're all ok after your ordeal, you're the only one I've yet to check over..."

It was a small lie, you'd not checked over Horangi either, though while you were waiting for König to arrive you did briefly see the Korean soldier walk by your office, he gave you a rather enthusiastic wave and you could tell just by looking at him that he was, for the most part, fine.

"...and Soap mentioned you looked a little stiff, so I had him fetch you." You could see Königs eyes narrow through his hood at the mentioning of Soaps name and you inwardly prayed that your mentioning the Sergeant ratting him out to you wouldn't cause any tension later on.

"This is not necessary..."With a huff König attempted to excuse himself and stood back up from the bed, deeming it a waste of your time and his, but before he had time to get anywhere you stopped him.

"Stop right there." He paused in his tracks and for once stared directly at you, his expression unreadable. You approached him, your tone level and professional.

"Raise your arms above your head."

"...What?" The enormous soldier tilted his head in confusion at your request.

"Raise your arms above your head." You repeat, your tone stern but your expression sympathetic.

Königs grey eyes flicked from you around the room, his voice seemed to get stuck in his throat as he attempted to worm his way out of the situation."I...I-I mean."

You took a few paces towards the mountain of a man and placed your hand against his forearm, his muscles instinctively twitched at your touch. "You can't, can you?" You gestured back over to the bed, your eyes soft. "Please, König. Let me take a look."

At this point König wasn't sure what to do or say, his eyes shifted between you and the bed that separated the two of you. You honestly thought for a moment that he would bolt back out through the door, so it came as a great relief to you when the large soldier sighed heavily and plonked himself down onto the cot, wincing slightly on the impact as he laid on his back, his icy grey eyes fixed firmly on the tiled ceiling above the two of you.

"I'm going to have to cut through your shirt to get a better look, is that alright?" You asked quietly, wheeling yourself back over to his side after laying out some supplies.

König gave you the slightest nod before focusing back on the tiles above your head. Carefully you cut away at his shirt, silently marvelling at just how toned his muscles were and feeling your cheeks grow warm.

Eventually you cut far enough up to be able to assess the damage and you were surprised König had been walking around at all. Dark black and blue bruising littered the right side of his rib cage and the already inflamed skin was peppered with what looked to be shrapnel shards which were still oozing blood sluggishly.

"Oh my God, König, why didn't you come and see me as soon as you got back!?" He didn't say anything at first, simply turning his head away from you and muttering something quietly in German.

"Well? König this is serious!"

"I ...I didn't want to be a bother." He looked back at you and stated simply, swallowing thickly as he noticed you holding a pair of tweezers. You breathed a deep sigh, your annoyance leaving you instantly as you looked at the man laying before you. You realised quickly that staying angry at him was extremely challenging. You placed a hand on his side lightly, readying your equipment.

"Just...Hold still, ok?" Little by little you begin the painstaking process of removing the shrapnel pieces embedded in the Austrians side. For the most part König stayed silent though you noticed the odd twitch in pain every so often and were sure to apologise to him while you worked. Eventually you were convinced that you had all of the pieces out and grabbed hold of a small cotton ball which you soaked thoroughly in antiseptic, König gave the cotton ball a withering look, all too aware of what was about to happen and no doubt regretting coming to see you in the first place. You gave his arm a reassuring pat and smiled, "I'll try be as gentle as I can."

The moment the antiseptic touched one of the deep wounds on Königs side the man's giant hand immediately grabbed your arm, his grip was like a vice and was trembling from the intense sting of the cleaning solution invading his injury. For a moment you weren't entirely convinced that he wouldn't snap your arm clean in half accidentally.

"Scheiße! S-sorry!" The moment König realised that he had grabbed ahold of you he recoiled away, afraid that he'd hurt you. His eyes wide in both pain and fear for your own well-being rather than his own as he scrambled to attempt at backing away from you in order to give you room.

You were quick to reassure him that no harm was done, giving your hand and fingers a wriggle to show he'd not hurt you. The relief in König's eyes that he's not crushed your fingers to dust had your heart bleeding over how much of a nervous wreck he actually was despite his imposing stature.

"It's ok, honestly, König! I'm fine, I'm just more concerned about you right now. Honestly I still can't believe you've been walking around the base like this!" You paused and sat back, watching quietly as König calmed down and settled back into a more relaxed position on the examination bed.

"I know you don't like doctors, I mean really, who does? And I know it hurts, I promise you I'll try to be as quick as I can be, all I need you to do is try and stay as still as possible for me, think you can do that?"

König seemed to stare at you in deep thought, fully absorbing your words before sighing heavily and relaxing back onto the bed again. You soaked another cotton ball in the antiseptic and give the soldier a reassuring pat on his hand. "Ready to go again?"He didn't reply, instead just opting to give a stiff nod.

The rest of the cleaning process went relatively smoothly, König stayed quiet and seemed to be making extreme measures not to move an inch while you did what you had to. When you finally put down the last cotton ball and made him aware you couldn't help but smile as the large man audibly sighed in relief.

"Oh come on, König! Surely it wasn't that bad?"He ran a hand over the top of his hooded face in pure exasperation and gave you a withering yet slightly warmer look than he had done since first meeting you. Were you maybe getting somewhere with him? Finally?

You laid a gentle hand on the back of his wrist"We'll leave it there today, ok? Normally I'd check you for broken ribs too but I'd say you've been through enough of my scrutiny today."

You pulled yourself away from your patient and rifled through your drawers, taking out a small orange bottle of pills.

"Take these for the pain, avoid heavy lifting and combat practice for AT LEAST two weeks. We got away with not having to stitch you up and even without checking I'd wager you've broken a rib or two."

König slowly stood and grabbed the bottle gently from between your fingers. His expression was unreadable through his sniper hood, though looking at his eyes you could see he looked calm, almost soft. The hulking soldiers glacial grey eyes narrowed almost imperceptibly, though this time more akin to a small smile rather than in the usual suspicion that you were used to from him.

"Danke..sorry, thank you, doctor. I...I will try and stay out of trouble."

You gave him a warm smile and a nod as you watched him walk steadily back out of your infirmary, he gave you one last glance, raising his fingers slightly in a tiny wave before disappearing around the corner.

It might've only been a minuscule amount, but you were extremely happy with the progress you'd made with your mysterious Austrian patient.

Chapter 8. Snakes & Ladders

E dited 22/05/23 - spelling and grammar changes. Minor additions to dialogue.

The next few days you were kept busy filling out copious amounts of paperwork. Sadly, the young soldier you'd tried desperately to keep stable had passed away in the night. His injuries were simply beyond healing.

Runner and Bolt. You'd had little dealings with either of the young men who had died as a result of the last mission, but your heart still felt extremely heavy for them and their families. Despite your attempts at not doing so, you took every loss as a personal failure of your skills as a medic.

You'd just finished writing up the last soldiers collection papers when you noticed an unmistakeable figure skulk past your door. You pushed yourself along the smooth flooring on your chairs wheels, coming to a halt just after the entrance to your infirmary.

"König?" He briefly paused then turned to face you, his posture slumped and tired, certainly not in keeping with his usual stance.

"Ja, doctor? I-is there something I can help you with?" The soldiers voice cracked a little from lack of use, it was evident that König only really spoke when he actually had something worth while saying and wasted very little time with small talk.

You gave a warm smile, beckoning him over as you pushed off from the floor to glide back into your infirmary on your desk chair. A moment later the mountain of a man stepped through the open doorway, giving the back of his neck a brief nervous rub, he regarded you for a few seconds before tilting his head slightly in confusion.

"Do..you need something, doctor?"

You smiled and shrugged lightly."Please, call me Dove, there's really no need to be formal around me. And truthfully? No, I don't really need anything from you."

You studied what little you could see of Königs expression and noticed him raise an eyebrow from behind his hood in confusion. Evidently he had expected you to actually have a reason for grabbing his attention, though the fact you didn't hadn't seemed to annoy him like your previous encounters.

"I've not seen you since I initially patched you up a few days back, I just wondered how you're finding your recovery so far?" You propped your head up in your hands, elbows resting on your knees as you smiled warmly at your colossal patient.

The Austrian didn't seem to need much time to think on his reply, "es ist langweilig...uh, what I mean to say is, it's...rather dull. Boring."

"Boring?" You replied in amusement.

The huge soldier huffed slightly and gave a nod. "Ja-Y-yes. I'm to do no training while I recover, correct?"

You smiled and hummed in confirmation."Mhm. Yep, that's correct."

"Then that is why it is boring."

König leaned on the doorframe, not quite committed enough to sit down with you but not really showing any signs of leaving either. You couldn't help but feel a little bad for the big guy, he had every right to feel bored. In between missions the entire base entertained itself by daily drills and fitness routines, with König's proverbial wings clipped that left the huge Austrian with shockingly little to do to actually entertain himself. Thankfully you knew just the thing to occupy his mind, atleast for now.

"Hey, feel free to say no, but if you're that bored d'you fancy playing a game with me?"

Königs head perked up slightly, "A...game?"You nodded your head quickly, "Mhm! Come take a looksy"

You opened a filling cabinet by the wall and pulled out a few different board games which you'd brought over on your transfer. They'd always come in handy on your past bases to keep your longer term in-patients occupied while they were bed bound and figured the logic on this base would be in different.

"What you reckon? I've got Snakes n' ladders, Hungry Hippo's, Mouse Trap...any of those float your boat?"

You watched as the colossal man pushed off from the doorframe and stiffly trudged over to you. He seemed to weigh up his options for a moment before nodding briefly to Snakes and Ladders.

"Ah! A fine choice! You know how to play?"König scoffed lightly, "Of course."

You grinned in response and set the game up, grabbing the dice and giving it a rattle around in your fingers as you watched König fidget with his little coloured counter which was to be his character marker.

"How's about we up the ante with some new rules?"

His grey eyes flicked up from his little character marker, which quite frankly looked fucking minuscule in his hands.

"New rules?"

You gave a nod "Mhm! Step on a ladder and you get to ask your opponent a question about themselves and they have to answer. Step on a snake and you have to be the one to answer the questions."

You watched as König glanced down at the board game, suspiciously eyeing up how many snakes there were and shifting his weight awkwardly from one boot to the other. For a moment you thought he wouldn't bite, but he surprises you yet again.

"S-sure. I think we can do that."

You clapped your hands together in excitement, causing the huge soldier to jump slightly."Awesome! Ok. Pull up a chair and get ready to lose!"

You couldn't help but watch König more than you did the actual board game, comparing how he was when you first met him as opposed to now was like night and day to you. Granted, he was still an extremely shy individual and still wouldn't engage in conversations with you first, but he was seemingly starting to handle the conversations you both had much easier than before and he wasn't giving one word answers all the time now, which was refreshing to say the least.

You rolled the dice, grinning as you landed on a small ladder and noticed how the Austrian tensed up a little.

"Hah! Question time...hmmm what to ask..."

You watched how König began to play with his fingers, his leg bouncing slightly at the thought of answering any question you had. While it was true that it was a good exercise to get to know each other you certainly didn't want to ask anything that would cause König to shut down and go back to ignoring you again.

"I've got it! What's your favourite animal?"

You did well at hiding the grin threatening to make its way onto your face as you observed Königs expression. The man sat straighter, one of his eyebrows raised in confusion and surprise, you knew he'd expected you to ask an invasive question and seeing the visible relief radiate off of his body was wonderful... and also kind of adorable.

He huffed out a small laugh from under his hood, "Uhm...well I guess it would be a Wiedehopf...Scheiße how do you say it in English...a little bird with funny red hair and a zebra coloured body."

You had no idea what this birds name was in English that König was trying to describe to you, but listening to him attempt was extremely sweet, you'd have to have a look on your computer later on to see if Google gave you any hints.

"That sounds like a beautiful bird, König." You replied with a smile on your face and you watched as his eyes narrowed slightly as he returned the smile back.

"O-oh they are! I would see them all the time in the forest near where I grew up...a-anyway it's my turn to roll I think."

You played a little longer without incident until you landed on a snake and watched as Königs eyes lit up slightly.

"Ah! I ask you something now, right?" You grinned and gave a nod. "Sure do! Ask away."

The soldier leaned back on his chair and bounced his leg while he thought about what to ask. You used this time to study his body and posture, he had to be one of the most toned men on the base and you couldn't help but feel an instinctually warm feeling in your stomach which you were quick to push down.

"Ok I've got it. Why do they call you Dove?"

You smiled and leaned over to grab the dice, "It's just a nickname that stuck with me at my last place. I was always known to try keep the peace, I'm a doctor, after all. Doves are, like, the OG symbol of peace!"

König chuckled at your response and shrugged "Yes I suppose you are right."

You continued playing the game, each time König landed on a snake or you hit a ladder you'd ask him some general questions. His favourite colour, food and the origins to his own callsign, which turned out to be "Red", "Mushroom soup" and "because I was the best at what I did in the Kommando Spezialkräfte and it stuck with me when I joined KorTac."

God you had so many other more prying questions you wanted to ask this man, his real name for one, seeing as it wasn't on any files or paperwork that you had access to. Eventually the game came to a natural finish and you were delighted that König was the one to reach the goal first.

"Well look at that, big guy, you won!" You gave him a congratulatory pat on the back before gathering up the game and packing it back away into the cabinet. You could tell by what little you could see of his face that König was very pleased to have won. He raised out of his chair to his full height, giving his wristwatch a quick glance.

"I must be going. Don't want to disturb you more than I have already. B-but..." He paused, shifting his weight from one foot to the other.

"Thank you. That was...very enjoyable. I'm not so bored anymore."

With that, König gave you one last polite nod and walked out of the infirmary, leaving you with a very big smile on your face and the beginnings of butterflies in your stomach.

Sure it had taken way longer than with any of the other soldiers, but you were finally working your way through the armour he had built up around himself.

You took it as a huge victory.

Chapter 9. Play Fighting

- -

E dited 23/05/23 - minor corrections to spelling and grammar.

-

The following weeks were relatively peaceful, other than the men being sent on general nearby scouting missions you thankfully had very little to tend to in the way of injuries, save for the odd sprain or graze.

You'd spent the morning sat around attempting to find something for you to do when you heard a commotion from down the hall. At first you considered just ignoring it, if there was one thing you'd become accustomed to it was the various odd screams and shouts of the men generally acting fools around each other. This time probably wasn't any different.

"Roach, hurry up! I think he's actually gonna do it this time!"

A young soldier that you didn't recognise ran past the infirmary door with Roach following soon after at a slower pace,"Psh yeah right, it'll end how it always does."

You stood up from your desk, quickly pacing over to the door and waving to Roach to grab his attention. He smiled and gave a slight nod,

"Good morning, Doc, you good?"

You gave a nod and gestured in the direction that the other soldier ran towards.

"Morning, Roach, what's all the fuss?"

Roach gave a sigh and shrugged rather nonchalantly."Oh, that? Price figured healthy competition between 141 and KorTac would strengthen bonds when we first merged together, what with us initially being at loggerheads n' all."

"Healthy competition?" You repeat in a questioning manner.

Roach gave a nod. "I guess it's been out of ear shot each time we've held one, but every week we have a sparring match to see who's the strongest and to keep us on our toes, so far König is undefeated."

Your eyes widened slightly, "König?"

The soldier nods again, "The very same. No one's been able to make him tap out yet, the dudes a fucking machine. Guess it doesn't help that he's built like a fucking tree."

Without waiting to hear your response Roach gave you a quick salute before jogging down the hall towards the sound of cheering voices. Immediately you followed the same direction that he took and upon rounding the corner into the mess hall you felt like you'd been suddenly plunged into a makeshift underground fighting pit.

All of the chairs and tables had been gathered up and stacked to one side, the operatives from both the 141 and KorTac had formed a ring around two men in the centre of the room who, at a first glance, looked to be trying to kill each other.

You hopped up onto one of the unstacked chairs to stand above the sea of soldiers in front of you to get a better look, what you saw, quite frankly, was terrifying.

Ghost and König, had each other in a headlock and both seemingly were at an impasse. The two men were drenched in sweat and the floor was smeared in what looked to be droplets of blood. The most alarming thing to you however, was that König wasn't wearing the sniper hood that you'd seen him in every other time.

The man was fucking beautiful.

His dirty blonde hair was tied up into a messy bun atop his head, you guessed that if he didn't have it tied up it would be around shoulder length and a few stray strands of it were hanging in front of his face. A large scar ran over the bridge of his nose and onto either side of his cheekbones, it almost acted as a contour to his features and a light smattering of dark stubble graced his equally scarred chin. Even with the blood freely running down his evidently busted lip the man looked like a fucking god.

Ghost, having had enough time to gather some strength while in Königs headlock, twisted his body weight. He grabbed König by the wrist he was using to keep the British man in place and dived to the floor, taking the much larger soldier down with him. You visibly cringed at the angle Königs wrist bent at due to Ghosts manoeuvre, though it seemed to do very little to stop the Austrian from a counter attack.

König wrapped his hand around Ghosts shirt collar, his enormous bicep flexing as he lifted the British soldier into the air. Ghosts boots were scrambling inches off of the ground in a desperate attempt to get some sort of security and traction. König raised his competitor another few inches and you could see the intense look in his eyes as he prepared to slam Ghost into the hard tile flooring beneath them.

You covered your mouth with a hand, your heart felt like it was about to beat right out of your chest in seeing your enormous Austrian patient perform his finishing move.

Except he didn't.

Somehow through all of the chaos and noise König had spotted you through the crowd of soldiers. You supposed that you stuck out a little more with being on top of a chair, raising you higher than the rest of the audience.

Königs icy grey eyes seem to stare at you in shock, almost becoming unaware that he was holding another entire man off of the ground. It wasn't until Ghost seized his chance that the Austrian came to his senses, and by then it was too little too late.

Using his powerful legs, Ghost kicked forward, one of his boots making direct contact with Königs right side. It had been a few weeks now since you patched him up and the lacerations from his last missions ordeal had healed, however you did suspect he had fractured at least two ribs also, and they would take far longer to heal.

Regardless, the look in Königs eyes told you that what Ghost had just done hurt like an absolute motherfucker and the huge man was quick to double over with an audible groan, grabbing his side and dropping Ghost flat on his arse. The British soldier stood to his full height, about to beat König into submission once and for all when a familiar bell sounded through the tannoy system, calling the fight to a complete halt.

"Look alive, lads n lasses. To the briefing room, chop chop."

Prices thick British drawl crackled over the speaker and immediately soldiers began to filter back out of the mess hall. Once the crowed had thinned enough you hopped off of the chair and made your way over to König, who was being hoisted up by Soap. Ghost lifted his mask just enough to unceremoniously spit some blood onto the floor.

"I'd have fuckin had you if it weren't for Price." Ghost grumbled, shoving his way past you and König and slinking out towards the briefing room with Soap in tow.

You frowned at Ghosts lack of sportsmanship, not even bothering to check if König was alright before he left. Taking another careful step forward, you gently placed your hand on the Austrians back, his attention snapped to you instantly and his glacial grey eyes bore into you with an intensity you've not seen from him before.

"Was tun Sie hier?"

He registers your confused expression before you even have a chance to ask him to translate, "What are you doing here."

It was more of a statement than a question and Königs usually calm voice sounded far sharper, more strained. The enormous man painfully stood to his full height, towering over you and for once you were the one feeling anxious rather than him.

"Roach mentioned you guys fight each week to bond with each other? I...I just figured I'd come check out what all the fuss was about, especially when I heard your name."

You see Königs tense expression waver upon hearing your reasoning, though truthfully you had every right to be there to watch without any real reason, you were no less a member of the team than every other soldier there. The huge soldier blew a loose strand of hair away from his face and rubbed his stubble anxiously.

"I just...I did not expect to see you in here, doctor...especially not watching me. You...you caught me off guard."

You couldn't help but smile gently, casting a brief eye sympathetically to how König was now holding his side.

"I'm sorry if I distracted you, König. It wasn't my intention, but please, if you're nervous about me watching you then don't be. I thought you did incredible. I've never seen anything like that before, I can see how you earned your callsign. King of the fight ring hm?"

You give König a gentle reassuring pat on his arm before turning to leave the mess hall, the Austrians expression was unreadable, though you could have sworn you heard a breath leave him as his jaw went slack at your response. It made you question when the last time König was actually complimented by someone.You turned around just past the door, noticing that König hadn't moved an inch.

"Don't be late for your briefing with Captain Price. You know where to find me if you need me to take a look at that..."

You gesture to the way he is guarding his side before giving a polite wave goodbye and heading back to the office in your infirmary, desperately trying to remain professional despite just witnessing two huge, sweaty muscular men throw themselves around in front of you. Not to mention seeing how smoking hot König was without his usual sniper hood.

You hissed out a sigh, desperately trying to think of anything else while you chastised yourself mentally.

Keep it together, Dove. Keep it together.

Chapter 10. Pain Bonding

Edited 23/05/23 - minor changes to spelling and grammar.

It was early evening by the time you started to see signs of life around the base again, clearly Captain Price had just about wrapped up with his mission briefing and had dismissed the squad.

Up until now you'd been trying to keep yourself busy by cleaning the infirmary and filling out paperwork when you heard a soft knock on the door, you tore your gaze away from an email that had just come through to saw an all too familiar gigantic figure awkwardly staring at you. It seemed König had taken up your offer and come to get a checkup after his sparring match with Ghost. You noted immediately that he'd put his hood back on and instantly found yourself missing his face.

You gestured immediately to the gurney and without needing any further instruction, König sat down stiffly onto it.

"All go well with the briefing?" You ask simply as you gently ease König out of his shirt, involuntarily marvelling at every ripple in his muscles as you finally worked his clothing away from his torso.

König nodes his head in response to your question, his voice exceptionally quiet in comparison to how it was just a few hours earlier after catching you watching him spar with Lieutenant Ghost.

"I-I can't say much, but yes, it went well I suppose."

The large soldier sat patiently on the bed as you grabbed your desk chair and wheeled yourself back over to him. You eyed his wrist in suspicion, remembering the awkward angle that Ghost had bent it during the sparring match.

"Both hands out in front of you, please."

König was confused at first but did as he's told and placed both of his hands on his knees. You could see swelling on the wrist that Ghost flipped him over with and the skin on both of Königs hands was scuffed and grazed around the knuckles.

"You really don't pull any punches, do you?" You muttered under your breath as you took one of his hands into your own. It was like holding a grizzly bears paw compared to how tiny your own hands were.

You gently felt around your huge patients wrist, probing for fractures, Königs fingers twitched slightly when you pressed on a tender spot but other than that he remained silent. You laid his hand on your own knee as you leaned to one side and grabbed a small roll of bandages. You could feel Königs palm sweating against your leg and your soul made an "aww!" sound at just how adorable and nervous this man was.

"Good news is it's not fractured, I think the weight of Ghosts fat ass just sprained it."

You grinned as König huffed in amusement, his fingers twitching as you lifted his hand up into your own again and begin to bandage his wrist. After a few moments his hand was suitably stabilised and you gave him the go ahead to take his hand back though at first he didn't seem like he wanted to.

Königs hand lingered on your own for the slightest of moments before he blinked himself out of his daydream and lifted his wrist up to observe your handiwork, wiggling his fingers to test the comfort.

König tilted his head slightly to one side and you could tell by the narrowing of his eyes that he was smiling, "Thank you, Doctor Dove."

You grinned, "Just Dove is fine, König, I've told you before there's really no need for formalities. We're friends, right?" You swore you heard a faint chuckle leave Königs mouth as he clasped his hands together and fidgeted awkwardly.

You pulled yourself away from simply observing the huge man's anxious tendencies and focused on actually being the doctor that he needed you to be. Though seeing him in all of his shirtless glory made the task extremely difficult.

You gently gripped Königs forearm, lifting it to one side a little so you could get a better look at his ribs. To say they were black and blue would be an understatement, the whole right side of his torso looked absolutely fucked. Despite Königs apparent growing level of comfort towards you there was still the telltale signs of pain and discomfort etched into his body and on his eyes. A thin sheen of sweat stuck to the man's scarred skin, his huge body stayed almost stone still as if any minor movement would cause pain, which you didn't doubt was the case.

"Lay down if you can please, König." Your tone is gentle and sympathetic as you watch this huge mountain of a man stifle a groan as he laid back onto the medical cot, the sheen of sweat growing ever more noticeable along his skin.

You gently hooked your hands around his right bicep, carefully lifting it as far above his head as König could comfortably stand to allow you to get a proper look at the damage.

"I'm gonna have a little feel, ok? I'll be as gentle as I can but it's going to be uncomfortable."

König snorted in frustration at your warning, covering his eyes with one arm and tapping his boot impatiently off of the end of the bed.

"This isn't necessary, honestly."

You're surprised and slightly amused by his quiet but sulky tone, it was akin to having an enormous child sitting on your bed.

"If it's not necessary why did you come to the infirmary in the first place?"

"Because you told me to." He replied simply, his eyes still covered by an arm.

You place a gentle hand on his side and his entire body tensed at the touch, you left your hand stationary for a moment to get him used to your physical presence before gently beginning to probe along each rib.

"If memory serves me right I didn't tell you to come to the infirmary at all..." your lithe fingers continue their work, observing how König twitches every now and then.

"What I actually said was if YOU wanted your ribs looking at then YOU know where I am. And here you are. So don't give me that bullshit."

König huffed sulkily as he lifted his forearm away from his eyes to peer at you, his grey eyes studied your face for a few moments and you could tell he was desperately trying to think of some sort of witty comeback. It didn't happen.

After waiting for a reply that evidently wasn't going to happen you opted to change the subject slightly, deciding to push the boat out a little with Königs comfort level.

"You know you don't have to wear that around me."

You gestured briefly to the sniper hood covering the Austrians face, noticing how the single eye you could see widened a little before he covered it again with his arm.

"I-I usually wear this."

"You weren't when you were sparring with Ghost." You replied in a matter of fact manner, causing your huge patient to immediately tense and choke on his air a little.

"Y-yes I suppose you're right. I don't wear it all the time like Ghost does with his...But I do generally prefer to wear it. It... helps with my anx-ngh!"

König hissed, doubling over and trying to grab his injured ribs, subconsciously swatting you away and trying to protect himself from your probing fingers. Immediately you grabbed his hand, drawing it towards yourself to try and stop König from doing any further damage to himself. The enormous soldiers eyes snapped to you, his breathing steadying slightly as you ran your thumb over the top of Königs hand in soothing circles.

"I guess we've found broken rib number one..." You chuckled quietly, hoping the little bit of gentle humour in your voice would aid to sooth your patient in some way. König seemed to regard you for a moment, his hardened gaze softening noticeably from behind his hood as he huffed out a small pained laugh.

"Ja..I think so." König settled himself slowly back into the bed so that you could continue your work, you made a mental note of which rib was broken before moving on to the next one down. Despite König now being relatively accustomed to your touch he still tensed up when you placed your hand back on him. For a while the two of you simply sat in silence, the large soldier allowing you to work uninterrupted other than the occasional growl of pain, which König was extremely quick to apologise for.

Eventually you'd fully inspected the right side of Königs ribcage and allowed the man a couple minutes to gather himself. You'd counted three broken ribs so far, the pain of a single broken rib alone was enough to completely floor a healthy civilian, let alone three. It was times like these where you truly appreciated just how tough the men you served along side actually were. Fair enough each soldier had their own unique quirks, but each and every one of them had been built from the ground up to be war machines. König was no exception.

"So this top secret mission that Price is sending you on, when do you deploy?"

You moved to the Austrians left side, beginning to gently feel your way across his chest to make sure he hadn't sustained any further unseen damage. König peered at you again from under his arm, his piercing grey eyes narrow in suspicion as he carefully processed your question.

"A week...why?"

"Because a weeks worth of healing with three broken ribs is worth jack-shit." You state firmly.

König scoffed, rolling his eyes. "I will be more than capable of carrying out my duties, doctor. I think you worry a little too mu-"

The huge Austrian seemed to choke on the air he was breathing before desperately attempting to clear his throat. To begin with you simply figured that you'd stumbled across another fracture. It wasn't until you'd glanced down and noticed your hand firmly resting on Königs chest and your fingers brushing lightly against his nipple that you put two and two together. Immediately you jerked your hand away and pretended to search for something on the table next to the two of you. Honestly you didn't dare to even attempt to glance in Königs direction and you didn't want him to see just how red your face had gone.

From the corners of your peripheral vision you could see König painstakingly pull himself up from his laying position on the bed. You could feel his icy grey eyes burning into you as you continued to focus on every other thing around yourself except him. Eventually you felt the heat had left your face just enough to turn back to face him without the risk of looking like a beetroot. You gave König your most polite and professional smile before grabbing a thick roll of bandages and signalling for König to shuffle a little further towards the end of the cot, which he did so immediately.

"I-I don't think your left side sustained any injury." You inwardly cursed how your voice got trapped in your throat and you made a point to clear it loudly.

"Let me just wrap you up and then you're free to leave, alright?"

König lifted his hood a little to idly scratch the stubble on his chin, his eyes seemingly looking everywhere else but at you. You sat in front of him, gesturing for König to raise his arms up a little so you could properly bind them.

"Keep this bandage on, don't loosen it. I know it'll feel tight but it needs to be ok? Just while your ribs mend."

You could feel the huge soldiers breath on the top of your head as you continued to secure König's ribs, shooting him an apologetic glance every time a pained growl managed to slip past his lips.

"We're almost done, you've done so well..." Your voice dripped in praise, glancing up to see how König was now lazily regarding you behind his increasingly heavy eyelids and you could almost feel him leaning into the praise in your voice.

A sharp tug of you tightening the knot of Königs bandaged ribs soon brought the soldier back into the world of the living and you had to reassure the poor man that he'd not offended you when he let slip a string of what you assumed to be curse words in his own native language.

You stepped back, admiring your handiwork for a moment before flashing König a triumphant grin."All done! See that wasn't so bad, was it?"

The Austrian shot you a sideways glance and then looked down at the carpet of clean white bandages that were holding his injured ribs in place. "When you said the bandages would be tight...I did not expect this tight ..." König attempted to slip a finger between his skin and the bandaging wrapped around him but failed. You shot him a sympathetic look and handed him his shirt back as well as a bottle of painkillers.

"Sorry, König. They've gotta be super tight I'm afraid. Go get some rest, I'll be speaking to Captain Price tomorrow regarding your deployment for this next mission."

You saw the man's eyes widen from behind his hood as he quickly hopped off of the bed, grabbing his shirt from you and stuffing the painkillers into his back pocket.

"You're talking to Price about me?" Königs voice seemed to drop in confusion as he straightened himself up the best that his injuries would allow.

"Of course I am. You're not being deployed within the next week with three broken ribs, König." You could feel a frown creasing your expression as you craned your neck to stare back at the massive soldier. Evidently he didn't like your plan, his eyes narrowing in frustration.

"That is not your call to make, Doctor." König crossed his arms, hoping you didn't notice him wincing at the action of doing so. You puffed your chest out a little, clearing your throat in order to use your "stern doctor voice."

"I think you'll find that it's exactly my call to make. König, you are injured. How're you going to hold a rifle with a sprained wrist? How're you going to leap over walls or jump out of buildings with broken ribs?" You gestured up and down at the huge man, ignoring the sarcastic chuckle he let out over your apparent concern.

"I think you're overestimating what I'm going to be doing on this mission, doctor. No leaping over walls, certainly no jumping off of buildings."

König took a single step towards you and placed a heavy hand on your shoulder, giving you a reassuring pat before turning to walk away and out of the infirmary.

"Danke...Thank you, for this." You watched as König gestured to the neat bandages wrapped around his chest and wrist. "I will...see you around, ja?" You gave your head a slight nod, drinking up the sight of him for the last time you'd see your patient that evening. Königs eyes narrowed in a slight smile as he gave you a polite nod before ducking under the infirmary doorframe to leave.

"Bis später, doctor. Enjoy your evening."

Like the previous times, you were once again left alone and to your own devices. Your mind wandering almost instantly to the incident between the two of you earlier. The way Königs voice got caught in his throat as you accidentally brushed the sensitive spot on his chest, the heat rising from his rippling muscles that shivered under your touch...

It was at the point you wished that this base had some sort of chapel attached to it, because you sure as hell needed Jesus right now to help you deal with the manner of thoughts that had begun to seep their way into your subconscious.

Chapter 11. Restless Nights

E dited 27/05/23 - minor changes to grammar and spelling.

König softly shut his bedroom door behind him, leaning backwards against it briefly and sighing heavily before kicking off his boots and flopping onto the bed. The large soldier groaned in pain and frustration, his calloused hand resting idly on the heavy bandaging around his ribs. They hurt like hell and every breath that König drew in made his fractured bones grate painfully against each other.

The whole thing was bullshit. Sure, it hurt to move and sure every breath König took made him feel like bashing his head against a wall, but that was still no reason for Dove to go rat him out to Captain Price. König frowned, yanking the sniper hood from off of his face and tossing it sulkily off of the bed. The Austrian made a mental note to get up at the crack of dawn to make sure he got to state his case to Price before the doctor could. There was no way he wasn't going on this mission.

Idle times in the base were far more stressful to König than the majority of his missions were. Of course the imminent threat of being shot, stabbed or tortured to death was enough to turn the most hardened man's stomach, but for König? It was the only thing he'd known for years. The man had been built from the ground up to be the perfect military weapon, just like every other member of the 141 and KorTac. Despite his generally reserved nature, the thrill of being out on a mission and the threat of death fuelled König unlike any other worldly high he'd experienced throughout his years. But it was a high that came at an even higher cost.

It wasn't just coincidence that Königs psychiatric notes on his medical files were missing. König had, by the grace of god, managed to pull rank with the higher up KorTac officials and captain Price to lock all psychological evaluations and records away as soon as he found out that the 141 and his unit were merging.

Price, as the commanding officer, was the only person who had the level of clearance necessary to access Königs files fully. When Dove had checked the files they'd thankfully assumed the missing files in his records were due to the previous medics negligence. This, of course, wasn't the case. The soldier was thankful that Price had ensured his information wouldn't be made available to anyone, even the doctors, unless absolutely necessary.

It wasn't like König was given preferential treatment with his sensitive information, a few soldiers on the base had taken advantage of their rank and standing within the team to do the same thing. Lieutenant Ghost had none of his psychiatric details on display for Dove but had provided the doctor with the odd scrap of info for them to add to his file every now and then. Horangi has also opted to lock away some of his mental evaluation notes, though only the parts that concerned his gambling addiction.

König huffed loudly, his fingers running along the edge of the bandages. He closed his eyes, desperately trying to avoid the feeling of becoming overstimulated. The bandages were too tight, König involuntarily fixated on the feeling of the coarse material hugging his chest, how certain patches aggravated his bruised skin with an annoying tickle that König couldn't scratch for fear of causing himself further pain.

"sich beruhigen...breathe."

Königs eyes remained shut as he attempted to sooth himself in his native tongue, his mind focusing on the cooling feel of the duvet under him rather than the unbearably itchy crushing weight of the bandages smothering his torso. It wasn't long before he felt his heart begin to slow, the overstimulated panic ebbing away and leaving König to breathe a little better.

[REDACTED]"Evaluation shows patient suffers from severe panic attacks due to physical sensory overload. Handle injuries with extreme caution, sedate where necessary."

Königs mind briefly flicked to a section of his psyche evaluation and he couldn't help but scoff out loud. His inability to stop his mind from blowing a fuse throughout previous physical evaluations had failed him at almost every instance where he had needed medical attention in the past, to the point of making a conscious effort to avoid the last medic that Dove replaced...

So why was Dove any different?

König linked his fingers together across his chest and stared blankly at the ceiling above him. There was something about this doctor which made him a little less anxious. Dove was persistent in trying to get to know him, knew not to overstep any boundaries and, for the most part, seemed extremely gentle in how they took care of Königs injuries. Nothing like previous medical personnel the soldier had experience with in the past... even still, your insistence on keeping König out of action and grounded until he had healed was a little too much caring for the Austrians liking.

Königs icy grey eyes relaxed a little as he pictured your face while you were checking his ribs earlier in the evening, his huge body struggled to suppress a shudder as his mind brought back the way you touched him, albeit accidentally. König was, quite honestly, frustrated at how you'd seemingly managed to worm your way into his thoughts with seemingly little effort. It wasn't right, he was a soldier, a high ranking KorTac specialist who's very callsign had enemies trembling...yet here he was, legged out on his bed sporting a rather monstrous erection at the thought of your delicate hand brushing against his chest.

"Gott verdammt..."

□□ MEDIC □□

At the other end of the base you were having a similarly restless night. You'd finished up in the infirmary and had plopped straight into bed the moment you got to your room. Honestly your body ached, despite only seeing König today you were absolutely drained, it was as if spending any extended time with the mountain of a man sapped you of your faculties.

You placed your hands behind your head, using your interlinked palms as a cushion as you closed your eyes and planned out your coming day. First on the agenda was to visit Price and request that König be grounded until his injuries healed. You knew he wouldn't like it but it was necessary and the thought of him out there doing god knows what with his body in it's current state was absolutely something you couldn't bare the thought of.

König had insisted to you that he was perfectly able to perform as he needed to for this next mission, and truthfully you didn't doubt the honesty behind his words. König was a god damned war machine and he wasn't about to let a little pain get in the way of his objectives...but still, you were his doctor, allowing the man to go out there went against everything you stood for. Your job was to heal, not harm. König would just have to fucking deal with it and be in a mood with you for a little while.

You squeezed your eyes shut and sighed heavily, desperate to continue making your mental chore list for the coming day yet finding yourself continuously thinking back to Königs insanely toned body as you checked him over, the feeling of his muscles involuntarily twitching under your fingers...how his whole body seemed to shudder when you accidentally brushed against his nipple.

It was fine...this was fine...you were on a base crawling with stacked out, beautiful men, you were bound to get a little crush on some of them...it came with the territory...

Just focus on work. Focus. Breathe.

You felt the all too familiar swell of warmth in the pit of your stomach and instinctively crossed your legs, rolling onto your stomach and smushing your head into the pillow with a slap and a comically muffled groan of frustration.

"Of all the men on base why are we crushing for the near seven foot tall walking anxiety campaign."

Dammit.

Chapter 12. Agree to Disagree

E dited 27/05/23 - minor changes to dialogue, spelling and grammar.

The moment your alarm abruptly woke you from a rather restless night sleep you were up, dressed and quickly making your way to Captain Price's quarters. You'd sent the captain a quick email the moment König had left the infirmary to inform him that you needed to speak with him first thing in the morning, he must not have been doing much at the time because he replied back to you almost instantly.

You tucked a stray strand of hair behind your ear as you quietly padded down the hallway and to Price's office. You knocked on the splintering wood surface and waited to be invited in, you noticed a shadow blocking the light from under the doorframe and moments later the door swung open.

"Ah. Hallo, Doctor."

You were mortified to see that it was König that opened the door, his face uncovered. You'd only seen him once before without his sniper hood on and it was very briefly but you remembered every little detail about his features...So why seeing his face again made your chest feel like it was about to burst from the sheer excitement was beyond you.

The huge soldier leaned against the doorframe, his eyes half lidded and seemingly unimpressed with your presence. You made it clear to him the day before that you'd be talking to Price regarding Königs injuries and the upcoming mission.The fact that the sneaky fucker got up even earlier than you and must have arranged to speak to the 141 captain purposefully before you, quite frankly, boiled your piss. Did this great big Austrian idiot have no regard for his own well-being?

"Seems I'm popular today...'av a seat." Price sighed.The captain was laid back in his chair, one of his boots resting firmly on the table between you as he gestured to the seat in front of you.

For a moment you continued to study Königs face, your eyes narrowing slightly over how smug the Austrian was to have been first to visit the captain. You said nothing to König, giving him a curt nod and brushing past him to take a seat in closer proximity opposite Price.

Prices expression was unreadable as he regarded you quietly for a moment before reaching for his cup and take a long slake of his drink, it looked to be tea.

"Go on then?" Price muttered to you from behind his cup. Your tired eyes widened a little as you cleared your throat and got straight to the point.

"Sir, I'd like to request that König be grounded for this upcoming mission."

Price regarded you for a moment, his eyes seemingly flicking between you and König who was still stood behind you.

"And why do you think that's necessary?" The captain asked simply.

"Sir, the nature of Königs injuries will hinder his ability to hold a firearm as well as affect his overall reliability and consistency with the other team members who you've picked."

"That's a lot of big words this early in the morning, Doctor." Price sighed, causing you to straighten up a little in your chair.

"To put it simply, sir. Königs injuries aren't nearly healed enough to go out on a mission. I believe him going is putting himself and the soldiers who go with him needlessly at risk."

You felt a lump form in your throat as Königs heavy footsteps approached you from behind, it took everything you had to not turn around to look at his stupid stubborn beautiful face. You'd no doubt that he was pissed off at you, you were, after all, getting in the way of his job. But this was your job and you weren't about to let an injured soldier be given a clean bill of health to go out there and potentially get himself and others killed just because he gets restless being on the base.

"König and I have already had this discussion. He seems to disagree with you, doc."

Price's gaze flicked up to meet König and without further instruction the huge soldier stood by your chair, you could feel his steely grey eyes burning into the top of your head as he looked down on you. You didn't dare look up to meet his gaze.

"H-he can disagree all he likes." You fumbled on your words slightly, desperate to sound more authoritative.

"I am Königs doctor, just as I am yours and everyone else's who lives on this base. As the chief medical officer...well actually the only medical officer on the base. I am telling him and you that he isn't going on this mission, he can't move properly, he can't perform out there properly and he just...he's just not going and...and yeah that's final."

Ok, Dove, a little rough on the landing there but hopefully he got the point.

Captain Price raised an eyebrow as your rather passionate speech, running a hand through his beard as he seemed to consider your words for a moment.

"König, anything to add?"

You felt the huge soldier shift his weight from one boot to the other beside you.

"Nein. Nothing, sir. The doctor, evidently, is under the impression that we are of the same ilk as the rest of the military. You know us all well enough by now, captain. The 141 and KorTac do not let minor injuries get in our way."

You'd not heard König talk in this way before and honestly it made you nervous. Despite his generally quiet and polite nature when talking to you in the past, the soldiers tone when stating his case to Price was like listening to a completely different man. He was cold, professional and completely uninterested in the argument you were trying to make in order to keep him safe.

Captain Price studied both of you for what felt like forever. You sat staring at your clasped hands, not wanting to face the scrutiny of your commanding officer and absolutely not wanting to face how König was most likely looking at you.

"Seems we're at a bit of an impasse, aren't we."Price finally spoke, leaning back in his chair and rubbing the back of his neck.

"On one hand we've got KorTacs top man, who we need for this mission. On the other hand we've got the new doctor who's demanding he be grounded due to his injuries." The captain leaned forward in his chair and sighed heavily.

"How's about we improvise."

"Improvise?" You and König said simultaneously.

Price nodded. "Dove, you're combat proficient, yeah?"

You nodded immediately, "Yes, sir. Though I've not been on the field for over a year."

"Good enough for me. This is relatively risk free for you, doctor. So here's my middle ground: I need König for this mission. He's playing a vital role. You want to keep an eye on him. I'm assigning you as his handler for this mission, after which he'll remain grounded until you give him a clean bill of health."

Immediately you noticed König stiffen beside you, his fingers twitching in what you assumed to be frustration.

"Captain, I do not need a babysitter." Königs accent seemed to grow a little thicker as he almost growled at Price. The captain, however, wasn't interested in hearing anything more of what the huge soldier had to say.

"It's not up for debate, son. I trust you've nothing to say on the matter either, Dove?" Price eyes you suspiciously, half expecting you to start complaining as well. You knew better than to try.

"No, sir. While I'm not happy that König is going on this mission despite my express professional opinion for him not to, at the very least I can keep an eye on him out in the field, as well as provide any on site medical aid should anyone else need it."

Price seemed happy enough with your response, gulping down the last of his tea and clasping his hands together with a loud crack.

"Well I'm glad we came to an agreement that works for everyone, right, König?"

You finally dared to look up at König, the majority of his face hidden by his messy dark blonde hair, the Austrian didn't respond.

"König." Price repeated, his voice dangerously low.

You heard the mountainous soldier draw in a deep breath beside you, evidently calming the anger and frustration he was experiencing. Eventually he turned and walked to the door, stopping just shy of the exit.

"Ja, sir. Kein Problem." He left immediately after.

You pushed down the sinking feeling in your stomach, meeting the captains gaze, which had softened somewhat.

"Don't worry about him, he'll get over it. I'll send you through a copy of the mission brief to look over so you know the plan. If you need to dust the cobwebs off of your field work im sure one of the lads will be happy to help. We depart in five days."

You stood up, straightening yourself and gave Price a polite nod before excusing yourself to start your day in the infirmary.

Five days to get combat ready and shake the rust off...Ok, that should be easy enough.

Chapter 13. A Dangerous Thing

"Oh damn, so he's been avoiding you since then?"

"Yup. I've barely seen him and even when I have he's been quick to leave before I got to say anything to him."

"That's rough."

"Mmhm, you're telling me..."

You rested your head in the palm of your hand as Roach and Horangi finished the maintenance on their weapons. The two of them were joining you and König on the upcoming mission along with Ghost, who, honestly, you were quite excited to see in action...if not a little terrified.

Horangi hopped up onto the table he and Roach were using to clean and maintain their weapons and rested his hands on his thighs. The Korean soldier seemed to study your face for a moment before grabbing one of his rifles magazines and began loading it steadily with ammo.

"I know it's your job to look after us, but honestly Königs been in way worse conditions before and come out on top."

You glanced up at Horangi and rolled your eyes a little, flopping back into your chair."I've absolutely no doubt that he has, but it's my job to make sure everyone here is safe and if he's gonna be in a mood with me for caring then so be it..."

Horangi fiddled with the magazine in his hand, placing the final few rounds into it with a satisfying click. "I get that you're still pretty new here, and your whole thing is to stop people getting hurt. But you're forgetting something important."

Your eyes glanced up to meet Horangi's gaze."Oh? And what's tha-"

"We're the 141, biiiitch! The toughest set of bastards the military has to offer!" Roach was quick to cut into the conversation, which up until now, had been serious.

Both you and Horangi stared at the other soldiers rather enthusiastic outburst, Roach stared right back, his eyes flicking between the two of you silently before adding "Oh!...and KorTac too. I guess you guys can be badass with us."

Horangi shook his head and grinned, turning his attention back to you. "To be fair, he's got a point." You tore your eyes away from Roach, who was now excitedly polishing the barrel of his rifle, and focused back on Horangi. The Korean soldier didn't wait for you to ask him to elaborate.

"I think what Roach is trying to say is that both the 141 and KorTac wouldn't have the reputation we've got if we just sat around whinging and feeling sorry for ourselves every time we got hurt. We're the best of the best, we get out there, get the job done and don't let the usual protocol get in our way."

"Protocol?" You sat back in your seat a little.

"Being grounded for trivial shit." Horangi replied simply.

Your eyes widened for a second before frowning at the soldiers reply. "So three broken ribs is classed as 'trivial shit'" you sneer. "Is to König." Horangi shrugged before leaning forward, resting his elbows on his thighs.

"You think König got his callsign from sitting around and taking it easy every time he had a splinter? I've worked with him for a few years now, like I said to you before I don't know barely anything about his life outside of KorTac, but I do know this..."

You leaned in closer to listen to Horangi, his voice now much lower and serious.

"The things I've seen that man have to do and the things that man has seen? It's more dangerous to his health being grounded at the base with his own thoughts than out there doing what he does best."

Well shit, that was something you'd never considered before, and the more you thought about it the more it made sense. You'd looked over countless soldiers files in the past, familiarising yourself with every detail about them both physically and psychologically. It wasn't until you were transferred to this base that you became acutely aware that some of the soldiers had enormous blank spaces in their mental health portfolios. You'd never questioned it up until now.

"How many of you suffer from PTSD?"

The question slipped out before you had a chance to stop it and both Horangi and Roach stopped what they were doing, growing silent. "I-I'm sorry that came out quite blunt didn't it." You were quick to raise both hands in an apology. Roach gently placed his rifle down onto the table and approached you, leaning against the corner with a huff.

"More of us suffer than those that don't." His voice was quiet, a faraway sadness hinting at his features briefly before he met your gaze and gave you a goofy smile. "That's why we're better off keeping busy! Right, Horangi?"

The Korean soldier smiled and nodded. "That's right."

Whilst neither soldier had told you outright, you understood now why König seemed so eager to be sent out on mission after mission. Immediately the more things began to add up you felt a crushing guilt in your chest. Technically you really had no reason to feel guilty at all, it was your literal job to stop the soldiers in your care from being injured or killed...but knowing that König relied so heavily on being given purpose on missions made your heart sink at the thought of taking that from him, injuries or not.

Honestly this was the first time in your career that you'd felt so conflicted about trying to keep someone grounded.You pushed yourself away from the table and rose to your feet, Roach and Horangi both looked at you expectantly.

"I think I need to speak with König."

Horangi offered you a warm smile as he begun loading ammo into a new magazine, he was evidently satisfied that you'd pieced two and two together without him actually having to spill any gruesome details of what König was like to live with on extended rest periods. The Korean soldier gave you a final nod as you went to exit the room, calling your name just before you disappeared out of sight. You turned back to face him, noticing his expression was a little more serious.

"If he's anywhere at this time of day then he'll be in the gym. Just...tread carefully, alright?"

You gave a slight smile and polite nod in response before disappearing around the corner and down the hallway, your nerves already building in the pit of your stomach at the thought of trying to make peace with König.

You needed to say what was on your mind before the missions commencement, there was only a couple of days left and you much preferred the idea of being handler to a giant mentally unstable soldier who actually liked you rather than one that wanted to snap your spine over his knee.

□□ MEDIC □□

The closer you got to the gym the heavier your boots felt. This was ridiculous, it felt like you were walking to your fucking execution rather than to have a civilised conversation. Eventually you got to the gym, you heard König before you saw him.

The echo of his fist slamming into one of the sand punching bags was akin to thunder which radiated through your chest and further worsened your nerves. You peered through the glass of the door, part of you hoped that Horangi had been wrong and that König wouldn't be in the gym. Horangi was right, and you cautiously observed as the huge soldier knocked the shit out of the sand bag in front of him, his back to you.

Drawing in a steadying breath you slowly opened the door, cringing inwardly as the action of doing so made the old doors hinges screech in rusty protest.

König immediately glanced over his shoulder, his icy grey eyes narrowing slightly when he realised it was you. The soldier immediately turned back to face the punching bag, seemingly uninterested in your presence. Swallowing down your nerves you quietly paced over to where König was training and sat on top of a stack of weights to the side of him, he gave you a sideways glance as you came into his peripheral vision.

"Come to ground me from working out too?"

You bit your tongue at König's rather childish statement, reminding your-self of the reason why you'd come to see him in the first place. You kicked your feet out in front of you a little, your hands clasped together on your lap.

"No, actually. I just came for a chat." You stated simply.

Another huge bang echoed off of the gymnasium walls, making you flinch as König's fist connected hard with the punching bag. He offered you a swift sideways glance in between punches and gave you a brief shrug when your eyes met.

"Well? You want to talk, ja? So talk."

With one final and extremely hard strike to the punching bag, König took a step away, grabbing a towel and wiping down his face. Your eyes eagerly drank up his features before he grabbed his sniper hood from off of the bench beside him and slipping it back over his face. You couldn't help but feel disappointed.

"I... I came here to speak to you about what happened the other day and...and to apologise."

You noticed Königs icy grey eyes widen slightly from behind his hood, his head tilting a little in confusion. "Apologise?" The tone in his voice was instantly much softer than it was when you first entered the gym. You nodded in response, rubbing the back of your neck to steady yourself.

"Let me start by saying I don't regret going to the captain regarding your injuries. I'm your doctor, first and foremost above all else. You were and still are, injured..."

König crossed his arms, shifting his weight from one leg to the other. Obviously he was still waiting for the actual apology part of your apology.

You drew in a breath, remembering what advice Horangi had given you earlier when you were sat together. Tread carefully.

"I was so caught up in following my own protocol that I didn't consider the fact that breaking protocol is essentially what this entire base does on a daily basis...and I didn't consider how maybe keeping you grounded would be more damaging to you than actually just letting you just go on missions...so for that I'm sorry."

König's expression was unreadable from behind his hood, you really wished that he'd not put it back on so that you could at least take a stab at what he was feeling.

The large soldier studied you for what felt like forever, his gaze burning into you as he idly rubbed his injured ribs. Eventually he sighed heavily, taking a step towards you and sitting by your side. It was only a moment later that he removed his face covering, letting it drop to the floor. Evidently he had only put it on when he noticed you earlier just to be moody, apparently he was over it now.

König drew in a deep breath, his lungs now unhindered by his sniper hood. The soldier ran a hand through his messy blonde hair, tucking a few stray strands away behind his ears. He regarded you a moment longer before giving you a gentle smile.

"ich weiß...I-I understand and I'm sorry too. I think maybe I've been a-"

"An awkward, sulky asshole?" You grinned.

"I...was going to say that I might have been a little difficult over the past couple days...but ok.." König gave you a withering look before grinning.

"I need to shower. Come find me in an hour or so, I'll go over the mission briefing with you."

"I've been over the brief already." You state simply, a polite smile stretched across your face.

"Not with me you haven't."König huffed out a small laugh, standing up and heading towards the exit.

"See you in an hour, handler. Don't be late."

-Authors Note-

Thank you so much to all of you who've read and commented so far. It means so much to me! This is a slooooooow burn story but we're getting there! Oh also, the cover art for this chapter is how I imagine our sweet anxious boi, König!

I do hope he's to your liking. I might try and make each chapter cover a different drawing from a scene in the story. If I do then I'll make it known in another A/N and you can have a look through the previous chapters to see the art Thank you my darlings. Now on to the next chapter....

Chapter 14. Here's The Plan

- -

E dited 30/05/23 - minor changes to spelling.

-

Come on. Just knock...how hard can it be?

You'd been stood outside König's door for the past five minutes, staring into the splintering wood that separated you from the huge Austrian solider. König had instructed you to stop by after he'd had chance to wash up from his training routine so that the two of you could go over the mission brief together.

It made sense. While you'd read through the mission statement a hundred times over at this point, you'd not done so with the one person you were acting as a handler to. For the most part the briefing stated the objective and general placements of the individual team members, they'd no doubt been given a much more in-depth run down before you became involved. It was nerve wrecking...but exciting.

With a sharp breath you knocked a cheery beat into the wood of the door, taking a step back and smoothing down your t-shirt. You fiddled with your fingers absentmindedly, desperately trying to find coping mechanisms for the storm of butterflies growing in your stomach. After a few moments you heard the door unlock and open, König was stood on the other side. ..and he looked fucking gorgeous.

The Austrians usual messy bun was lacking, his dark blonde hair hung freely and framed his face, still obviously a little damp from his shower. His glacial grey eyes seemed to glint in an almost predatory way, further enhanced by the dark circles he'd gained from an obvious lack of sleep. Königs face seemed to light up when he noticed it was you, despite inviting you to his quarters in the first place, he seemed almost relieved and surprised to see your face.

"Ah, Doctor! Please, come in."

König grinned and held the door open for you. You squeezed your way in between him and the wall, soaking in the sight and smell of his room.

It was a simple enough dormitory, smelling faintly of coffee and sandalwood. A shelf containing various books in both English and German were stacked neatly and you smiled when you noticed that some were comics and magazines on video games. Königs bed was meticulously made, the file containing the mission briefing was sat in the middle of the duvet.

Given there was no sofa or extra seating in his room you gathered that Königs bed would act as the makeshift desk to go through the mission.

König shut the door quietly behind the two of you, pacing over to the bed and rubbed the back of his neck anxiously as you both took a seat on the bed. The huge soldier made sure to sit a good arms length away from you, not wanting to encroach on your personal space. He shuffled back into the bed, crossing his legs and flicking open the folder that was positioned between you both. It seemed that he didn't want to waste any time with small talk.

"Ok...so... scheiße where do we even start with this?...How familiar with the mission are you, exactly?"

You crossed your legs, mimicking König and leaned back against his wall.

"Only what's in the folder, really. I don't know where everyone's going to be positioned, only that we're looking for more leads to do with an arms dealer?"

König nodded, humming in response to your answer. He flicked the file open, scrubbing through the pages until he came to a topographical map of the area the team would be conducting the mission around. König grabbed a pen that was tucked into the rings that bound the folder together and started drawing small circles with initials next to them, which you recognised to be each team mates first letter of their callsign.

"Alright, so, Ghost and Roach are entering at point A, sooo...right here." König marked a small area of the map with a "G" and an "R". "They'll be doing the heavy work on this one, so it should be pretty easy for us. Horangi is going to provide backup for them both over at point B...here."Again König marked the map, this time with an "H".

Your eyes didn't leave the page, studying every detail that König marked down. After a while the map looked like a child had scribbled all over it, though the large soldier looked rather pleased with the diagram he'd drawn up for you.

"Now that just leaves us, doctor."

Königs accent seemed to get a little thicker as he addressed you. Your gaze meeting his directly for a moment before flicking back down to the map, studying where his index finger was pointing to.

"We're all the way out here. Just you and I."

You tilted your head in slight confusion, though König seemed to already have an idea of what you were thinking.

"We don't need to be too close to the action. A sniper. That's my role in this mission."

Your eyes widened in admiration, the expression didn't go unnoticed by the large soldier. "You're a sniper? That's amazing, König...I've heard that being a sniper takes insane skill. I...I just didn't expect you to have that kind of role in the mission."

"Because I'm zu groß? ...Too big?" König responded, an eyebrow raised as he rested his head in his hand. The amount of times he must have had this reaction made you feel a little guilty.

"It's not all I do, generally I act as an Insertion Specialist."

"An insertion specialist?"

"Ah...the team battering ram, I suppose." König rubbed at his broken ribs idly, a shy smile playing on his lips.

"Again, that sounds insanely interesting. Truthfully I didn't know much of what anyone on the base did as far as roles went. If you're an insertion specialist as well as a sniper, does that mean there's other snipers on the team so you can interchange roles?"

König grinned at your enthusiasm for learning more about the work he did, leaning back against his beds headboard and propping himself up onto some pillows.

"Nein- uh, no, I believe I'm the only one here currently with a sniper title on their official documents. B-but that is not to say that the others aren't good shots too! Lieutenant Ghost is an excellent marksman." König seemed quick to add the last part in, almost out of fear of coming off too confident in his own abilities. The man really needed to learn to give himself credit where it was due.

After all, he was unlike anyone you'd ever met before.

▢▢ MEDIC ▢▢

Despite only coming to Königs room under the pretence of getting information about the mission from him, something which should have been relatively quick, you'd been there for almost three hours.

Every question you could think to ask König was sure to answer. Granted, it might not have been personal questions that you really wanted to know about him, but the fact the huge soldier was giving you so much of his time was a blessing in itself.

Throughout the course of the evening you'd gone from sitting at opposite ends of the bed, flicking through the mission folder, to shuffling closer together. Neither of you had really noticed it had been happening until you leaned back and your knee brushed against Königs. The soldiers icy grey eyes flicked down to the physical contact instantly, though he didn't mention anything or adjust his own position to pull away from your touch.

"So at first you were told you couldn't be a sniper?" You hugged your legs, eyes wide with curiosity.König nodded and hummed an affirmative sound.

"Mhm. Couldn't keep still."

"You do kinda need to be still to be a sniper." You grinned.

"Hah! Ja, you do indeed."

"But you did it in the end, so it's all good, right?"

"Mmhm, its all good." König playfully mimicked your own accent, grinning at you before wincing as he sat up a little, the pain in his injured ribs stabbing at his side. You instinctively got into your doctor headspace, flipping yourself over onto your knees and facing König directly, concern etched into your features.

"You ok, big guy?" Your hushed voice dripped with worry, though König quickly tried to downplay the situation.

"Please don't worry, I'm fine. Maybe training so hard was a...poor choice." The Austrian gave you a sideways smile, his eyes widening slightly when he noticed you shuffle further towards him and gesture to his t-shirt.

"Can I see?" You asked quietly, noticing the way König stiffened ever so slightly at your question, even without his mask on his expression was unreadable. "Don't worry I'm not going to run to Price again and get you grounded, dummy." You rolled your eyes playfully, smiling as Königs muscles relaxed a little at your reassurance.

You took the man's silence as permission granted and gently eased Königs t-shirt up just enough to see his ribs, the toned muscles were still very bruised, though in the week since breaking them you were pleased to see the thick blackness of the original bruising had become more of a lighter bluish purple.König was healing at what appeared to be a steady rate.

You laid a hand gently against Königs side, enjoying the heat that radiated off of him and the feeling of his strong muscles under your fingers.With an almost feather-like touch, you felt along his bruised ribs, pleased with the progress he was making. You continued to check over him in silence, your hand ceasing movement and your eyes flicking up to see Königs face when he shuddered slightly, an almost whimpering sound escaping his throat.

"I-I'm sorry, I didn't mean to hurt you." You whisper apologetically.

"You didn't." König chuckled, tucking a hand behind the back of his head.

You tilted your head in confusion slightly, raising an eyebrow question-ingly as you placed your fingers back at the same spot on Königs side and brushed against his skin lightly. The huge soldier shivered again, a grin threatening to stretch its way across his face despite his obvious attempt at looking serious.

"Oh...no way." A devilish smile creased your lips.

"What...?" König raised an eyebrow as he stared up at you.

"The biggest, baddest guy on the base is ticklish?" You grinned.

The soldiers eyes widened, staring straight through you for a second before he shook his head quickly. "Nein." "No?""Absolutely not." He grinned ."I'm calling bullshit." You giggled as your fingernails scratched lightly at Königs sensitive skin, still being mindful not to press on his bruising.

For a while König seemed determined to prove you wrong, he stared intently back at you, his expression unwavering...until his eye twitched slightly and you noticed him tensing the muscles in his jaw in an attempt to stop himself from smiling.

Eventually König grinned, holding both of his hands up in an act of surrender as he squirmed under your touch. "A-alright! Alright! I give up!"

Hearing this man laugh, genuinely laugh, was just about the sweetest sound you'd ever heard. You didn't ever want to see or hear him sad again.

In an attempt to get away from your probing fingers, König kicked one of his legs up, attempting to use his knee as a barricade between you both...That had been his intended plan, anyway. But things don't always go as we plan them.

By the time König had raised his knee to separate the two of you, you'd already sat on his leg, something which he must not have noticed. The

Austrian, being not only insanely bigger than you in general but near on infinitely stronger than you, ended up lifting you up while you were sat on his leg.

The end result was you being propelled forward and onto his chest, your face literally a couple of inches away from his own.

You both stared wide eyed at each other. Neither of you quite knowing what to do or where to go from here. You drank in every single detail about Königs face, the way his stubble didn't grow around the deep scarring on his chin, how soft his lips looked, the way his celestial eyes seemed to dart across your own features to study you intently. You could feel his heartbeat hammering against his chest as you lay on top of him, it warmed you to the most primal part of your very core.

"I...uh...es tut mir leid...Sorry, let me just..." König almost whispered to you under his breath, you had to stifle a small gasp as you felt the soldiers large hand snake it's way behind your back to help push you back up off of him.

Quickly you regained your senses, trying and failing to climb off of the Austrian with some of your grace intact. Eventually after much shuffling and wriggling around, you managed to roll yourself off of Königs bed, smoothing down your shirt and pants in a desperate attempt to look a little less flustered.

König sat up and shuffled to the end of the bed, holding his side lightly as he did so.

"You sure you'll be ok when we're going out?"

König raised an eyebrow. "Going...out?"

"When we go out on the mission." You clarified. "You're sure you're well enough?"

"O-oh! Ja-yes, I'll be fine, honestly. Do not worry yourself. We're far away from any real danger, remember?...or have you forgotten our role in the mission briefing already?" König stood, towering over you and folded his arms in amusement. You grinned, giving him a playful smack on the side of his arm before turning your head to face the door.

"I...I should get going. It's late and you need to get as much sleep as you can."

Königs expression dropped slightly, obviously disappointed that you had to leave. Knowing he's enjoyed your company made your heart feel like it was glowing. The soldier squeezed past you, standing by the door and opening it when you got within close enough proximity to him.

"Gute Nacht, süße Träume."

"Good night?" You attempted to translate, earning a warm smile from König, who nodded slightly.

"Mhm. And sweet dreams." He almost whispered.

You gave König a gentle pat on his bicep before turning and walking down the hallway to your own sleeping quarters.

"Goodnight, König."

Chapter 15. Snowblind

0500 hours. Time to get up

You'd been awake and staring at your clock long before the alarm told you it was time to get sorted. Today was the day of the mission and you'd have been lying if you said you weren't nervous.

You quickly got out of bed, haphazardly putting your basic gear on while you brushed your teeth. You'd not seen König since spending time with him in his room and if you were being honest with yourself, you'd not stopped thinking about him. The ripple of his muscles under your fingers, his melodious laugh...you'd committed every ounce of him to your memory.

Soap had come to see you on your way for a successful mission, catching you the minute you stepped out of your dormitory. "Excited?" He grinned, making sure your gear was buckled up and secure. "Nervous." You replied, smiling back as the Scotsman placed a helmet on top of your head and slapped the top of it playfully.

"You'll be fine, doc. Stay on Königs six and let him do his thing, you'll all be home before you know it."

"Yeah, I suppose so. Thanks, Sergeant." You grinned, following the man outside and across a dead space of land where the helicopter was waiting to drop you and the team off at the mission. You could already make out the distinct shape of Ghost, Horangi and Roach, the three men conversing with one another while they waited for you...and apparently König too, who wasn't anywhere to be seen.

"Good morning, guys. Ready to do this?" You asked in your most cheery voice, hoping they didn't hear how nervous you actually were.

"Born ready!" Roach beamed.

"Always." Horangi nodded his head, his tone a little more reserved than usual but still warm to you.

"Mhm." Ghost simply grunted, his pale blue eyes scanning over your face briefly before looking back towards the base. You followed his line of sight, noticing he seemed to be looking at the same door I exited from.

"Where's König?" You asked the question before you had time to check your tone and your obvious level of excitement caused Ghosts gaze to snap back over to you, his eyes narrowing slightly.

"On his way." Ghost grumbled, again breaking eye contact with you to stare off into the distance. A sudden weight bared down on your shoulder and you turned to see it was Horangi leaning on you, the Korean soldier dismissed Ghost's grouchy mood and chuckled from behind his own face covering.

"The day König shows up before the rest of us will be a miracle. The man is always last on the heli."

You couldn't help but grin at Horangi's words, almost imagining König running around frantically in his room to get ready in a panicked rush. The majority of times you'd seen him you'd picked up on little things that further solidified this theory, the most consistent thing being Königs inability to threat his belt through all of the loops on his pants. There was always one loop he missed...not that you'd been staring at his pants for extended periods of time or anything.

It was no sooner that you wondered when exactly König was that you spotted an unmistakable silhouette approaching the heli through gently falling snow. König was kitted out in a full tactical gear and he had a large sniper rifle slung over his back. You couldn't help but feel disappointed seeing his face, or lack thereof, hidden away by his sniper hood. You'd never seen him full kitted out in his mission gear before and he looked...intimidating.

"Good morning!" You give your most cheery voice as the mountain of a man walks straight by you.König shot you a quick glance, giving you a simple nod to say good morning before boarding the heli with Horangi, the rest of the group quickly got on board shortly after. Apparently he wasn't in the mood for pleasantries.

You'd been up in the air for the better part of an hour now and the majority of that time had been spent observing König, who was sat at the opposite end of the helicopter. The man didn't meet your gaze once, his attention solely focused on staring out the window. Occasionally Roach would shout something over to him and he would reply with either a one word answer or just not at all, you noticed his leg bouncing slightly.

"He's always like this on a mission, don't worry about it." Horangi seemed to read your mind, sliding his balaclava up over his nose to take a drink of water and shooting you a reassuring smile.

"He looks so nervous." You almost whispered to the Korean, afraid König would hear you over the constant whirring of the choppers propellers. Horangi have a single loud laugh and grinned, shaking his head.

"Hah! Nervous? No, look closer."

You followed his advice, fully allowing yourself to drink up your team mates posture and behaviour, your eyes widened a little.

"He's...excited?"

Horangi nodded, leaning into you, you helmets bumping together slightly. "It's the only thing that gets his heart racing. It's a shame he's not on Insertion today, else you'd be in for a real treat." You give a half hearted smile, glancing back over to König, you knew he was a soldier, obviously, and a very talented one at that to be a part of KorTac...but the thought of him being so excited to kill people just didn't sit right in your stomach.

"Right. We all know the plan?" Ghosts gruff British accent cut through your train of thought, the rest of the team looking to him as he laid out a map onto the floor of the heli, you recognised it from the mission briefing folder you'd been given from Price.

"Me and Roach are taking point, we'll get in there and flush out the target. Horangi, you'll provide backup." Ghost turned his attention to you, gesturing at both you and König.

"König and his babysitter will waiting up top, when we draw out the target you get'em."

You frowned at the Lieutenant's jab at you being Königs babysitter. You were more than that, you were the only doctor for the entire base, a literal life saver. Certainly not just some annoying hitchhiker on the teams back.

It wasn't long before Ghost and Roach were given the signal to drop, the two men jumped from the heli a couple miles away from the target base. It wasn't long before Horangi was given the signal to jump too. The Korean gave you a reassuring slap on the shoulder, leaning in so you could hear him.

"Remember to stay out of his way and don't interfere, you'll be fine, don't look so worried! Trust me!" You drew in a breath to reply to Horangi but the soldier dropped out of the heli before you had time. It was just you and König now, you could cut the tension with a knife.

□ □ MEDIC □ □

By the time you and König had jumped and landed the previously gentle snowfall was beginning to get heavier. You cut yourself out of your parachute, eyeing the huge Austrian as he did the same thing. König glanced over his shoulder to you and then silently gestured to the top of the large hill that you were sat at the foot of.

Due to the huge difference in height you struggled to keep up with Königs walking pace at the best of times, but the deep hillside snow along with the steep incline of the hill itself made it almost impossible for you to stick by his side. By the time you reached the top of the hill you honestly felt like you might throw up in your mouth a little from how much your lungs burned. König hadn't waisted any time from the moment he touched down and hadn't waited for you...or even checked to see if you were still behind him on the walk up the hill. You figured he was completely in his headspace, though you couldn't help but take it a little personally that he'd not once checked to make sure you were ok.

When you got to the top of the hill König had already set up his position, hugging the ground next to a large evergreen shrub caked in snow. He observed the surrounding area through his rifles scope, his steady breath making itself visible to you from the small frozen clouds which occasionally huffed out from under his face covering.

"So...we're staying here?" You asked quietly, watching as your companion remained completely still, not moving to acknowledge you in any way. "Y es." He responded simply. "For how long?" You responded, kneeling down and hugging your knees to keep warm. "Until the job is done. You know this." There wasn't any hint of amusement in Königs voice, his entire tone was cold, professional, nothing like when he was at the base.

The two of you remained laid in the snow for well over an hour, waiting on König to be given the signal to begin prepping to take the all important shot.He prepared, steadying his breath as he shuffled down a little more, further sinking into the snow which was rapidly growing around him.

Before König is given the all clear you hear the distinct sound of gunshots through your earpiece, followed by shouting in both English and Russia n."This is Ghost, Roach has been hit. I repeat, Roach has been hit. Going on alone. König, get ready, you'll only have one chance."

Your eyes widen as you hear Ghosts gravelly voice over the radio, your heart sinking as you absorbed what he had said. Roach had been hit? The Lieutenant hadn't bothered to elaborate on his team mates condition over the radio, but you knew any form of injury all the way out here was bad news. You had to do something.

Standing quickly, you waded through the thick snow and gathered up your pack containing as much first aid supplies as you could feasibly carry. König broke away from his scope, immediately standing up and grabbing your arm when he noticed you about to run down the hill.

"What the hell are you doing!?" The huge soldier hissed at you, his icy grey eyes burning into you with an intensity you'd not seen from him before.

"You heard Ghost. Roach has been hit, I'm a doctor, König. I can help him." Your voice is gentle but stern as you try to pry his large hand off of your shoulder.

"You have your orders, Dove. You are not going down there." Königs accent was thick, his grip on you tightening.

You stared deep into his eyes for what felt like forever, searching for something, anything that you could say or do to help make the situation better for König. You rested a gloved hand on Königs forearm, his intense expression faltering slightly at your touch. You drew in a steady breath, your grip tightening on Königs arm. He'd hate you for this.

"I have to. I'm sorry."

Königs eyes widen in surprise, unable to keep a proper hold of you as your small frame quickly ducks under his arm, twisting away from his grip. You daren't look back as you sprinted down the hill towards the enemy base, your mind racing between König and Roach.

"I'm sorry, König. Please be ok, Roach."

"Nein nein nein! Shit!"Back up on the hill, König had gone into crisis mode and was frantically pacing back and forth in the snow.

Between the sight of you running down into enemy territory and Ghost literally screaming down his earpiece to take the shot, he didn't know whether he was coming or going.

König stared at his rifle for a moment, weighing his options before turning his attention back towards the direction you'd ran off in, his knuckles were white from balling his fists up so hard. The man had two choices: he could stay on the hill, take the shot and kill the arms dealer....or he could miss the only chance he had and run down the hill and hope to catch up with you before you got yourself into some serious issues.

"Gott verdammt..."

König drew in one last deep breath to steady himself, mentally apologising to Ghost as he pulled his earpiece out and silenced it before sprinting down the hill in your direction.

All hell was about to break loose.

Chapter 16. Blood And Ice

You near sprinted down the hill, trying desperately not to fall in the thick snow as you followed the sounds of gunshots and shouting. Evidently the mission hadn't gone to plan and you'd taken it upon yourself to at least make sure the men got out relatively unscathed.

You kept expecting to hear the unmistakable crack of Königs rifle firing at his target but it never happened, which even with everything going on right there and then, made you worry for your companions safety.

Eventually you reached the base, your feet carrying you so fast that you practically ran into the side of one of the buildings, your back pressed against the icy cold wall as you peered around the corner to survey your surroundings and assess the danger. Call it lucky, but the hostiles didn't seem to be in your immediate area, allowing you to step out of cover and inspect the nearby area. Eventually you came across a smeared splash of blood in the snow and tracks that evidently showed someone has been dragged into a dilapidated old store room nearby.

Armed with nothing other than your backpack of medical supplies, you quickly and quietly approached the run down little building, your hand pausing just before you grabbed the handle.

The moment you stepped over the storeroom threshold you heard the unmistakable sound of safety being taken off of a weapon. Your eyes scanned the darkened room, eventually falling on a figure laid in the corner who had an assault rifle pointed directly at you.

"Roach...?" Your voice was gentle and steady as you raised both hands up in a submissive gesture.

The dark figure seemed to falter slightly upon hearing you speak, shuffling into the light of a nearby window slightly. You felt a rush of relief when your suspicions were confirmed, the figure was Roach.

"D-dove? What're you doing here!?"

You ran to Roach, pulling him into a relieved hug. The soldier chuckled quietly, pushing his face covering up and off his head so he could see you unhindered. He returned your tight hug before pushing you away to look at you, worry and pain was etched across his youthful face.

"Am I glad to see you, doc...but for real, why are you down here!? Where's König?" Roach almost whisper shouted at you, his hands giving you a quick shake.

"Königs back up on the hill, I couldn't just sit there when I heard you'd been hit." You explained, laying out a variety of supplies by your side as your eyes swiftly wandered over Roach's body, checking for injury. Eventually they came to rest on the young soldiers leg, his thigh was bleeding steadily from what looked to be a rather sizeable bullet hole.

"Can you move it at all?" You asked quietly as you gently cut away at the fabric surrounding the wound, trying to ignore how Roach bit back a groan when you peeled away some dried material which had stuck to the injury.

"Like hell. It was the Lieutenant that dragged me into here so I wouldn't be seen by anyone."

"Ghost?" You sounded surprised.

"Of course! He practically threw me in here and said he'd be back to get me once the job was done...here i am!" Roach grinned. Even in these conditions the soldiers almost childlike quirks made you laugh.

"You really admire him, hm? I've not spoken much to him, honestly...he doesn't seem interested in talking to me." You smiled gently as you grabbed a small pack of disinfectant, tearing the corner of it open with your teeth.

"Uhm, of course I admire him. He's the coolest guy in the whole milit-AGH!" Roach curled into himself, grasping at his thigh as you doused it in the antiseptic solution. You gave him an apologetic pat on his shoulder as you waited patiently for the soldier to gather his senses again. Eventually Roach leaned back against the wall and stared at you sulkily.

"Could've given me a little warning..." he muttered, crossing his arms like a sulking teenager.

"I find it hurts more when you know it's going to happen. Looks like the bullet went straight through, lucky you." You smiled gently and shrugged.

"Sure, lucky me." Roach retorted, rolling his eyes before seemingly pausing in thought and frowning. "He's gonna be so pissed at you, y'know."

"Hm? Who?" Your eyes briefly met the injured soldiers as you began wrapping some thick medical gauze around his thigh. Roach tilted his head to one side and raised an eyebrow."Who'd you think? König!"

Your hands jerked a little at hearing Roach say the Austrians name, the abrupt action causing the soldier to wince.

"You think so?" Your voice was quiet as you watched Roach shrug his shoulders.

"Well let's see. You've left Königs side, run down here into the middle of hostile territory...without your weapon by the looks of it, and essentially done everything you weren't meant to do while out here. So yeah, König is going to be super pissed at you..."

Your eyes widened slightly as you stared blankly for a moment. "Yeah I'd not thought about that..."

"Didn't think so." Roach grinned.

You shrugged nonchalantly, trying to act as if König being mad at you wasn't bothering you. "I'll have to deal with it when we get back. I'm not going to just sit around knowing someone needs my help, I'm a doctor, it's in my blood to help people who need it."

"Well said." Roach grinned, his toothy smile faltering slightly as you tightened the knot in his bandages to fully secure it.

The crackle of Roaches intercom caught your attention, hearing Horangi's thick Korean accent. You leaned forward a little, straining to hear what it was the soldier was saying to Roach. Eventually your curiosity got the better of you and you grabbed the earpiece from Roaches head and clicked the button on the wire around his neck which allowed you to speak on the open channel.

"Horangi, it's Dove. I'm here with Roach, is everything ok?" You spoke quietly, peering out of one of the nearby windows to see if you could spot any movement outside.

"Dove!? What the hell are you doing with Roach? Is König with you too?" Horangi's voice crackled over the radio, you were relieved to hear that he sounded his usual self.

"I heard he'd been hit and I had to come make sure he was ok. And no, he's not with me, I think he's still up on the hill."

"Ohhh he is going to be so pissed off with you." You could tell by his tone that Horangi was grinning.

You sighed heavily, pinching the bridge of your nose, "I know I know. I'll deal with it when we're all back home safe. Have you met up wit Ghost? Is he alright?"

"Yeah. We're both ok, don't worry. You sit tight, don't move. We'll come get you both on the-"Horangi was abruptly cut off by more gunshots over the radio, your heart sank to the bottom of your stomach as the radio was abruptly cut off. For a moment you just stared into nothing, your mind racing. You glanced over at Roach, the young soldier seeming to know what was running through your mind as he frowned and shook his head.

"Don't do it." His eyes were pleading as he watched you lean forward and reattach your pack of medical supplies to your back.

"I'm sorry, Roach. I have to. Stay here, alright?"

The soldier rolled his eyes and gestured down to his bandaged leg. "I don't have much choice. Please, Dove. Don't go, Ghost and Horangi have got this. Have a little faith in 'em."

You gently rested a hand on the thick gauze on Roaches leg, giving him a reassuring pat. "I couldn't live with myself if something happened to them that I could've helped prevent. I'm sorry, Garry."

Roaches eyes widened a little at the use of his real name rather than his callsign, he studied your features for a moment before sighing heavily and handing you his assault rifle. "If you're determined to go out there then at least go out there with some protection."

You hesitantly took the rifle from the soldiers hands and looked back at him in concern. "Thanks, Roach...but what about you? You gonna be ok here?"

Roach grinned, rubbing the back of his neck and giving you a brief thumbs up."I'll be A-OK, doc. Don't worry."

You gave him a smile in return before quickly throwing your arms around him for a swift hug."Thanks, stink bug. I'll be back soon."

▢▢ MEDIC ▢▢

Schieße where the fuck are you, Dove!?

Königs icy grey eyes frantically scanned the area, desperately trying to find any faint proof that you'd passed by through the area of the base he was now searching.

König ducked behind a shed, spotting two guards a few meters in front of him. The huge soldier unsheathed a black tactical dagger from his belt and held his breath, waiting for the opportune moment to make his move. The guards didn't get a chance to look at König, let alone defend themselves from him and soon enough he was moving past the two freshly deceased bodies to continue his search to find you.

A thousand terrible thoughts were ablaze like a wildfire in Königs mind. Had you been captured? Tortured? Worse? You needed to be safe, he needed you to be. Honestly he regretted ever agreeing to Captain Prices terms of allowing you to come along on the mission, in the back of his mind he knew something like this would end up happening and now, surprise surprise, there König was. In the middle of hostile territory. Searching for your sorry ass with nothing but a knife and thousands of KorTacs dollars in advanced weaponry left back up on the hill to get buried under the ever increasing snow. To say he was pissed off would've been the understatement of the year.

At this point König was frantically searching every room of every building he went past, leaving a string of carnage in his wake. The sound of his own blood pumping through his veins from the sheer adrenaline was almost deafening to him as he barged through the door of a small storage shed, his icy grey eyes instantly widening as they came to rest on Roach. The poor soldier very nearly squeaked in surprise as König immediately stomped over to him, his gaze quickly resting on the medical gauze tightly wrapped around Roaches leg.

"Where are they." Königs voice was cold, steady...down right terrifying. Roach held up both of his hands in an act of submission as he shuffled further back against the wall, desperate to create some space between himself and the huge soldier towering above him.

"I-I don't know."

"You don't know?" The tone in Königs voice made Roach wince.

"N-no idea! Dove showed up, gave me some first aid and left as soon as they heard Horangi and Ghost taking fire elsewhere in the compound!"

For a few moments König seemed to simply stare straight through the injured soldier, his eyes barely visible from behind his sniper hood and the unlit room the two were in. Eventually the huge soldier turned on his heels and marched back towards the door. For a brief moment Roach considered asking König to stay, to not do anything stupid. He knew better than to bother, and seconds later he was alone again, silently praying that this whole mission would just be over and done with.

König stomped through the flurry of snow, the visibility was getting worse with every passing minute and the sheer volume of snow muffled the sound of enemies nearby, though it did little to properly hide the sound of nearby gunfire. Dove was nearby, König could feel it in his soul. Now he just had to pray that he'd find you alive.

Eventually König came to a small area a little more secluded, the surrounding buildings acted as a shield from the brunt of the blizzard. It would've been a welcome relief for the Austrian if he didn't feel like he was on the brink of insanity.

König stood in the middle of the sheltered area, his eyes shut in absolute concentration as he desperately tried to pinpoint where the sound of gunshots was coming from. A more nearby shot was fired, helping König to make his mind up and immediately begin walking in the direction he heard it, only to stopped dead in his tracks.

A group of men were blocking the way, each of their faces completely obscured by thick winter clothing and snow goggles. König counted seven of them in total.

The enemy group began to fan out silently, circling König like a pack of wolves. König studied each of them with an almost lazy expression from behind his hood, noticing that none of them appeared to be carrying firearms...though that didn't mean they weren't armed with something.

The huge soldier stood in absolute silence, allowing the two men on his left and right to disappear from his line of sight. He waited, listening for the moment he heard the crunch of snow under boots close enough to him to act.

The man to Königs right was the first to go, his jawbone was crushed to splinters in Königs hand before his neck was snapped with such force that it echoed around the surrounding buildings. Next was the enemy to his left, too stunned to fully commit to an attack after seeing his team mates face crushed in front of him. He joined his friend in a similar fashion and fell in a twitching heap in the snow.

König sighed in annoyance, the vapour caused from his warm breath tapering out from the eye-holes in his hood. He cracked his knuckles and shook out the tension in his arms as the other five remaining hostiles glanced between each other, speaking hushed Russian to one another before immediately rushing towards König as one group.

The first of the remaining five to die was the man who charged König head on. The huge Austrian crouched down just as his attacker reached him, grabbing the Russian and raising him completely above his head before slamming the man's spine across his knee. The feeling of the young man's individual vertebrae crushing themselves to dust on impact brought a sickening grin to Königs face.

Four to go.

The next man went down with little effort, completely overpowered by Königs superior height and reach. The Austrian only had to land a single well placed strike with his knife to his assailants neck and before the man had time to comprehend what was happening he was gargling on his own blood.

Three left.

You'd naturally assume that the less people to handle in a fight would mean the fight itself would become much easier. As it turned out, it was the complete opposite.

König was beginning to struggle with keeping tabs on where each man was. The fallen bodies of the remaining men's comrades had significantly free'd up space in the small enclosed area for the remaining men to spread out. This needed to be finished and fucking quickly.

Whether it was a combination of a complete mental overload, the freezing cold of the blizzard or physical exhaustion, König was beginning to lag. The soldiers movements grew more sluggish, his bruised ribs aching, fingers numb from the icy wind.It was as if the remaining hostiles could smell the vulnerability of Königs position and they didn't wait to give him a chance to prepare.

The first man lunged at König with a knife, forcing the huge soldier to jump back and directly into the second man who latched onto Königs back, jamming a tactical knife directly into the side of the Austrians shoulder. The impact of the blade tearing through his skin took every ounce of air from Königs lungs and the soldier had to rely on sheer will power and adrenaline to stop himself from collapsing.

König spun on his heel, grabbing the man who'd stabbed him and, using his own knife, split the man's stomach open from one side of his hip to the other. The Russians hot insides were steaming against the icy ground.

"Hah! Pick your guts up off the floor."

Two left.

Authors Notes

Im so sorry this chapter has taken so long! I've been so busy at work and with general life that I've not had any time for much of anything! I've actually had to split this chapter into two parts, so part of it is already kinda pre-written and hopefully won't take long to publish! Anyway I really hope you enjoyed this chapter!

Chapter 17. Red Lullaby

EDITED 28/08/23 - HEAVY REWRITE. READ FOR UPDATED VERSION.

-

By the time you'd found Ghost and Horangi the brunt of the action had already passed. You ran up the flight of stairs of what you assumed to be the main building in the compound to find Ghost stood in the office at the top, his hand wrapped around the shirt of the now dead arms dealer while Horangi flicked through various files scattered on the floor.

The Lieutenants cold eyes snapped to your direction, looking you up and down before dropping the dead man he was holding onto in a crumpled heap on the floor.

"What the fuck are you doing here?" Ghosts heavy British accent grated against your already frayed nerves, as he stomped over to you, his heavy boots causing the splintering wooden floor to creak beneath him. You opened your mouth to answer but were cut off by Horangi giving a sharp whistle to get the Lieutenants attention.

The Korean soldier was holding a single sheet of paper in his hands and turned it to face Ghost, a gloved hand pointing at a certain section of the paperwork. "This asshole was just the tip of the iceberg...seems our friends have been getting imported firearms from Mexico, there's some kind of Codename here...El Sin Nombre."

Ghost continued to stare into your very core for a few more agonising moments before turning away to face his Korean team mate. "We need to show this to Price. This goes way beyond what we first thought."

"Right." Horangi nodded in agreement, folding the piece of paper and tucking it into one of the pockets on his vest before giving you a reassuring nod.

"Silver lining though, we get sent to Mexico to deal with this thing then we don't have to deal with this fucking snow anymore. Im quite looking forward to the sun." Horangi gave you a wink, noticing how you couldn't help but smile in response to his attempt to look on the bright side of things.

"Psh. You say that now but you'll be wishing for the snow when your frying your bollocks off in the fucking sun." Ghost grumbled under his breath, giving Horangi a quick hand signal to follow him outside. You followed suit, trying to hide the slight insult you felt at Simon not even bothering to look at you as he barged past and sauntered downstairs.

Honestly you were relieved that the mission was finally over and done with and all things considered it seemed to have gone relatively smoothly despite Roach sustaining injury.

Oh shit we need to go get Roach.

You jogged down the stairs trying to flag Ghost down and make him aware that you'd tended to Roaches injuries before finding him and Horangi. You hoped that Simon knowing that you'd helped one of his closest friends would give you at least a couple of good points in his book. Your train of thought on earning some minor approval from Ghost was cut short when you almost ran into the back of Horangi, who, along with the Lieutenant, was stood stone still.

You peered around the two soldiers. What you saw made your blood run cold.

Not twenty feet away stood König, the soldier was covered in blood which ran freely down his gear. He had a young man pinned under his boot and was holding the battered corpse of another man in one of his hands.

"P-please..." You could hear the strain in the still living mans Russian accent choke out as he weakly begged for his life under Königs boot.

"I-I have a famil-" The mans plea was cut short, you watched in horror as König crushed the mans head under his heel, repeatedly stomping down onto his face until it was completely caved in. He threw the corpse of the other man he was holding across the icy ground, leaving a bloodied smear as the body slid to a stop.

You took a step forward towards König, only to be stopped by Horangi before you could go any further. The Korean soldier gripped your shoulder and gave it a gentle squeeze."I wouldn't." His voice was quiet and steady. You continued to stare across the snow over to König, the man you saw in front of you wasn't the man you recognised. Not anymore. He was ruthless, a blood thirsty weapon of war. A feral creature. He was terrifying.

"We're only human." Horangi stated simply, his voice remaining quiet. "This is the price of war, Dove. The things we've seen, the things we've had to do. Eventually something in us just...snaps." You felt the Korean soldiers hand give you another reassuring squeeze as his words sank in.

Your body seemed to push you forwards between Ghost and Horangi before your mind actually registered that you were moving. If either of the soldiers called after you then you didn't hear them over the deafening sound of your own blood pumping in your ears.

Before you knew it you were stood behind König, the enormous soldiers back was turned to you and you became acutely aware that, in his blood-fuelled haze, he'd not noticed your presence.

Your tired eyes studied his massive form, noticing quickly that the blood König was saturated in wasn't just from the enemies he'd dismembered. The man was littered in slash and stab wounds which leaked freely from various gaps in his combative gear. The fact he was even standing at all was astonishing to you, even more so when you noticed the thick black handle of a tactical dagger embedded to the hilt in König's shoulder.

"König..?"

Your voice was little more than a whisper as you tried to grab the soldiers attention. König didn't move an inch, his bloodied body continued to stand stone still facing in the opposite direction. A gust of biting blizzard wind cut through the compound, catching the Austrians sniper hood and making it flap and lift a little. You noticed from what little you saw of the brief glimpse of the side of Königs face was also covered in blood before the change in wind direction caused his hood to fall back into place.

Against your better judgement you took another step forward, ignoring the way your body instinctively screamed at you to distance yourself from the near seven foot tall soldier who was, right now, seemingly in the middle of a complete dissociative and PTSD-fuelled breakdown. You swallowed down your fear the best you could before raising your hand, fingers twitching nervously as you moved to place a gentle palm on Königs uninjured shoulder.

The resulting action was near instantaneous, and nothing how you'd hoped he would react to your touch.

König spun on his heel faster than you had time to register, his huge gloved hand instantly gripped your throat with vice-like power as his icy grey eyes peered at you with a worrying lack of recognition. You felt the air being crushed out of your windpipe as the soldier held you in place, ragged and pained breaths coming out in uneven puffs of vapour from under Königs hood which drifted out from his eye-holes. The man looked possessed.

"K-König it's me..." Your voice strained through the grip he had around your throat, noticing how his fingers twitched ever so slightly upon hearing your voice before tightening back up again.

"D-don't you recognise m-me, dummy? C'mon it-it's time to go ho-" Your sentence was cut short has you felt Königs hand apply further pressure around your neck. At this point both Ghost and Horangi had taken up positions to the left and right of you both, you noticed from your peripheral vision that the Lieutenant was aiming his gun at Königs head, an action that hadn't gone unnoticed by Horangi.

"Ghost, what the fuck!?" The Korean hissed out, his accent thick as he desperately tried to avoid escalating the situation any further.

"Let the doctor go, soldier." Ghosts gravelly British accent cut through the howling wind of the blizzard, causing Königs cold eyes to briefly flick from you and over to Simon. The huge soldiers grip on you remained unmoving.

"You're going to make it worse, just stop." Horangis voice strained against his own instinct to scream at the Lieutenant. By this point the Korean soldier had worked alongside König for a little over two years and had bared witness to similar instances happening to his Austrian teammate, either when the odds were stacked against him or his brain had simply overloaded from the sheer number of horrors and atrocities König had both seen and committed.

König was a capable soldier, strong, dependable, completely fearless and most at home in the thick of battle where the darkness of his own thoughts would leave him well enough alone...but that didn't take away from the fact that, as much as he hated to admit it, he was only human and was not without flaws.

Whether it was Ghosts insomnia and complete inability to allow himself to get truly close to others, or the way Roach would use almost childlike humour to hide the fact he would sob most nights into his pillow. Every soldier of the 141 and KorTac alike had their limits and dealt with the stresses of their jobs differently.

This was the main reason why Captain Prices team were given special permission to redact and lock away certain psychoanalytic files from prying eyes. Even if those eyes belonged to the doctor charged with helping to monitor and keep them safe.

"This is your last warning, König." Once again Ghosts commanding voice cut through the sound of the blizzard."You don't let go of Dove and I'll put a round right between your fucking eyes."

At this point Horangi was pointing his own weapon over to the lieutenant, the respect and friendship he had for his fellow KorTac member now outweighing the chain of command that he had to follow while force-merged with the 141.

Things were going to shit pretty fast, your eyes darting between Ghost and Horangi before resting back on König. You needed to try and snap the big guy out of this fuge state by any means necessary...before König either crushed your windpipe or Ghost and Horangi shot each other.

"I c-can't believe you don't recognise me, dummy...and after we p-played snakes and ladders together too..."

Your voice strained against Königs gloved hand as you began to try bring him back to a more aware state, your own much smaller hand coming to rest shakily on his wrist.

"You remember that? Snakes and Ladders? That's how we learned m-more about each other... You told me your favourite animal is a...a Wiedehopf, I think you called them...y-you couldn't remember the English name for them...s-so I googled it...we call them Hoopoe's."

You felt the grip around your neck weaken by the most minuscule amount, Königs eyes were glued to you as you continued to gently ease him back into some semblance of sanity.

"Y-you also told me you love mushroom soup...d-do you remember that? You must do..."

You found a space between Königs sleeve and his glove and drew small, calming circles across the underside of the bare skin on his wrist with your fingertips. The enormous soldiers grip on your neck almost instantly slackened and you saw his cold grey eyes soften, the kindness returning back to them as König begun to come back to his senses.

"König...please...let's go home, ok? When we get back to base you can teach me how to make this mushroom soup you said you love so much...or we can just get S-Soap to make it for us seeing as he's always in the kitchen raiding for snacks, huh?"

Your undoubtedly bruised neck ached as you stared up at König. He was there, you could see it. König was coming back around, albeit slowly.

The mountainous soldiers hand had slid away from your neck but still lingered with his palm flat between your collarbones as you continued drawing the calming tickling circles against his wrist. Horangi and Ghost had both lowered their weapons in stunned silence, looking between one another.

"Missions over, ready to go home and play some more snakes and ladders with me, big guy?"

That last little comment was the final push König seemed to need to fully bring him back down to earth and ground him.His hand slid away from you and grabbed the shredded fabric of his hood, pulling it off of his head to reveal his beautiful face, which looked dangerously pale save for a black eye and a deep cut which had split one of the sides of his upper lip open.

"Y-you're safe?...I, I thought you'd...Mein Gott, Dove, im so happy you're ok..." König staggered forward, seemingly unaware of the damage he'd sustained as he enveloped you with his strong arms. You immediately buried your face into his chest, leaning into him and savouring his scent. Your eyes slid shut as you pressed yourself harder into Königs clothing, wishing deeply that it were his bare skin against your cheek rather than the tattered and bloodied combat gear.

"Good to have you back with us, chingu."Horangi's voice was warm as he approached you and König, his eyes giving you a brief glance to make sure you were ok before fixing themselves on the much larger soldier. Ghost remained where he was, while you couldn't see anything but his eyes it was evident that the lieutenant hadn't witnessed this side to König before, he was cautious and with good reason.

"Time to move out. This blizzards getting worse by the minute and we've still got to grab Roach. Horangi, make the call for extraction." With that, Ghost turned and headed out towards the direction of the storage shed that Roach was still inside.

□ □ MEDIC □ □

You'd thankfully found Roach where Ghost had originally left him, relieved that no other previously undetected enemies had walked in on him in his vulnerable state.

The bad new was, however, that due to the severity of the blizzard there was going to be an indefinite wait to be extracted. The helicopter simply could not navigate through such severe weather safely, so for now you were all stranded. You'd all opted to simply wait it out in the supply shed that Roach was situated in rather than to move him elsewhere unnecessarily.

At this point the cold had gone straight to your bones and you were struggling to sit without shivering violently. You weren't the only one, everyone was feeling the bite of the cold. Even Ghost, who barely showed much of any emotion, occasionally blew warm breath into his cupped hands to desperately try to warm himself up.

Despite the missions success the general vibe inside of the supply shed was icy- and not in terms of the temperature outside. The men were exhausted, freezing and still reeling from the stress of the day. The only one who still remained in reasonably high spirits was Roach, but that was nothing new. You shuffled over to the younger soldier, who hadn't appeared to move an inch since you first patched him up a few hours prior. The tight bandaging on his thigh was now stained with a deep crimson, which you opted to redress before extraction...whenever that would be.

"So the mission was a resounding success then, yeah?" Roach grinned, his voice staying quiet as he watched you work.

"I wouldn't say it was a resounding success, Gary...but yeah I think Ghost got what he needed." You shrugged, glancing over your shoulder to the Lieutenant who was leaned against the wall of the cabin, keeping watch through the dusty windows. Your eyes caught a glimpse of a dark patch staining the fabric around Ghosts bicep and as soon as you'd finished redressing Roaches injury you went to approach the Lieutenant.

Now trying to get Simon Riley to do any generic or menial task that he didn't want to do was near on impossible...Getting the man to give you permission to tend to his injury was another thing entirely and had to be approached with a delicate hand.

"G-Ghost, sir?" You mentally kicked yourself for the way your voice caught in your throat the minute his cold eyes stared at you. The Lieutenant seemed to regard you in the same way that cattle regarded flies. A fucking nuisance.

Ghost didn't respond to you at first, simply turning his head slightly more in your direction. He regarded you silently for a moment, waiting you to state your reason for interrupting his outside observations.

"I noticed you're hurt. Do you mind if I-"

"No." Ghost interrupted you before you had time to finish your sentence. "It's nothing. Go sort your boyfriend out."

You frowned as you felt heat rush to your cheeks at how Simon referred to König, your eyes instinctively flicking over to the Austrian who was slumped against one of the other walls of the shed. Whilst the mountainous soldier had been extremely relieved to see you were alive when he came to his senses, he was now quiet, on high alert despite his exhaustion and seemingly intent on avoiding conversation with you.

You turned your attention back to Ghost, shaking your head slightly and sighing."I'll deal with him once I've dealt with you. Now show me your arm." This time you weren't asking and Ghost knew it, he turned to face you fully, seemingly hoping his size and reputation would cause you to buckle and give up. It didn't. You watched as the lieutenant sighed heavily under his mask and unzipped his jacket, wriggling his injured arm out of its sleeve, the instant change of temperature brought goosebumps to his bare skin.

The wound wasn't overly severe, certainly not by Ghosts standards anyway. It appeared to be relatively superficial, caused by a bullet grazing his skin in one of the fire-fights he'd been through on the mission.

You carefully took Ghosts arm in your hands, dabbing at the wound with one of your pouches of anti bacterial you kept in your supply pack. You had no doubt it stung like a bitch, though there wasn't a hope in hell that Simon was going to make that known to you.

"So...we're all heading to Mexico?" Your voice was quiet so as not to disturb the other soldiers. Ghost regarded you for a moment, seemingly weighing up whether or not to tell you to shut up or to humour you for once.

"Might be.""I guess it depends on what captain Price thinks, huh?""Mhm."

Granted it wasn't much of a conversation, but at this point you were just happy that Ghost hadn't completely bitten your head off about you leaving your post with König. Speaking of which...

Your eyes fixated on König over in the corner of the room, the Austrians own icy grey eyes met you for a brief moment before he opted to stare at the wall instead. You sighed, turning your attention back to lightly bandaging Ghosts arm. The Lieutenant studied your handiwork briefly before giving you the slightest nod in thanks.

"Cheers. Now sort him out before he bleeds everywhere...or goes on another rampage."

Simon gestured over to the Austrian slumped in the corner and now that the adrenaline had worn off you had to thickly swallow your increasing anxiety over trying to explain to König why you'd felt it necessary to leave his side and jeopardise the integrity of the mission.

You inhaled deeply to steady your nerves as you approached König, kneeling down beside him and laying out your medical supplies. Somehow you figured you'd need way more than just some antibacterial wash and some bandages, but that would have to wait until you were all back home safely at the base. You only hoped that Königs injuries would hold out until the extraction...whenever the hell that would be.

Königs tired eyes met you briefly before they became unfocused, almost as if he was looking behind you rather than at you. Despite the Austrian not having the hood on his face his expression was dangerously unreadable.

"How...how're you feeling, big guy?" Your voice was small and gentle as you studied him closely. The poor man looked like he'd gone ten rounds with a combine harvester and lost. One of his eyes was showing the beginnings of closing up due to swelling, the bruising around his eye socket further darkened by the dark circles he always had from lack of sleep. The right side of Königs upper lip had been split open completely and you were inwardly horrified to see that when the light hit his face in a certain way you could actually see one of his canine teeth from between the split skin.

Various puncture holes littered Königs combat gear, some of which were stained with rich, dark blood. The most noticeable injury, aside from the knife protruding out of his shoulder, was a very large bloody patch to the lower side of Königs abdomen.

You laid out what little equipment you had left and shuffled yourself close to the huge soldier, his eyes narrowed slightly in tired annoyance.

"Look, I know you're pissed off at me for leaving your side earlier...but I need to help you, alright?"

Either König knew the extent of his injuries or he was simply too exhausted to try to stop you, whatever the reason was you were thankful when he made no attempt to stop you from examining the wound. You unzipped his gear and peeled his shirt away from the injury, by the looks of it one of the men had stabbed him and dragged the blade part way across one side of his stomach. It was a fucking miracle that his insides were still...well, inside.

"I had to do it, you know. I couldn't just sit around once I heard that Roach was hurt.""Bullshit." König spat, his eyes narrowing as he stared at you."You could have done your fucking job and stayed put.""My job is to save people, König." You frowned, trying your best to clean away the excess blood as gently as possible despite your annoyance.

"We went over the mission. You knew exactly what your role was, Dove. To to follow me. To do as I said and to stay out of the way. Heilige schieße do you even have any idea what could have happened to you? Do you even care!?"König sat upright, his body tensing as he lost control of his temper. At this point the other soldiers in the shed fell into stunned silence, even Ghost looked a little taken back by the Austrians uncharacteristic outburst.

Königs cold grey eyes continued to burn themselves into your very core for what felt like an eternity before he doubled over in pain and fell back against the wall, clutching at his injured shoulder with his good arm. Honestly at this point you couldn't even find it in yourself to be angry at him, it had been your fault that König was in this state in the first place. This bloodied up, beautiful idiot of a man had put himself through hell just to make sure you were safe. Not to mention he'd failed the only objective he had in the mission...because of you.

"I...es tut mir leid...I'm sorry, I just..."This time when you heard Königs voice it was much calmer, quieter. The way he looked at you now wasn't in annoyance but sadness. "I don't know what I would have done if something had happened to you..."

Your eyes widened upon hearing this and you couldn't stop yourself from leaning back a little and pausing what you were doing. Honestly you didn't know what to say or do at this point. Your gaze lingered on his features for a moment, desperately trying to read König. Despite how pale he was from the amount of blood loss you could see a slight blush warming his cheeks as he turned away slightly in anxious embarrassment.

Eventually your mind seemed to snap back into doctor mode and you cleaned up the nasty wound on his abdomen the best you could before tearing open the top of an antiseptic pouch with your teeth. You laid a hand on the top of Königs thigh, giving it a light squeeze to catch his attention, the soldiers gaze snapped to you instantly.

"The wound needs cleaning. I'm sorry, König, but this is gonna sting a little."

The huge Austrian stared at you a moment longer before his tired eyes flicked between the pouch of antibacterial liquid and the deep wound on the side of his stomach. König drew in a shaky breath and seemed to anchor himself a little closer to the wall before giving you a quick nod to do what you had to.

The events that followed the moment the thick stinging liquid came into contact with Königs wound would forever be etched into your mind...and oddly enough, for all the right reasons.

"Verdammte Schei-mph!?" The feeling of your lips against his own caused König to almost choke on his own air as you leaned into him and passionately kissed him. You stayed in that position, locked against his lips until his pained breaths began to settle and slow, the agonising sting of the antiseptic fading away and being replaced with a much more positive feeling.

You slowly tore yourself away from Königs lips, inwardly savouring every last detail on how he tasted and felt. You absently wiped some blood away from your mouth, the split in König's lip painting your own in a deep red. If the Austrian soldier wasn't blushing before then he sure as hell was now, his beautiful face almost appeared to be aglow with renewed vigour despite the fact he was still heavily injured. His expression was that of complete shock.

"Evac on route, pick up is in fifteen minutes. We need to move. Now."H orangi's voice broke through the crushing silence between the two of you and you had to give your head a little shake in an attempt to get back into a more professional headspace.

Just like that the moment was gone.

If you were being honest with yourself, in those last few minutes, you wished the blizzard outside would have lasted a little longer.

Authors Notes

Oh my goodness! A new chapter for you all! I know I said this one would be published a lot sooner but I ended up adding to it and it ended up being almost 5k words, phew!

Also I'm sorry this took ages! I'm a tattoo artist and winter hasn't been kind on the business, especially not in the UK where we have the "cost of living crisis" so I've been swamped with trying to get my calendar booked up!

Thank you all so much for your continued support! It means so much to me and hopefully I'll free up enough time soon to start on the next chapter...I see some fruity times on the horizon finally amiright heheheh.

- Moth

Chapter 18. A Vaulted Past

E dited 28.08.23: minor changes to spelling and grammar

PATIENT REPORT & EVALUATION Name: n/aAge: 32Patient I.D: 3721104Callsign: König

Knife wound to right shoulder caused complete dislocation of joint. Foreign object removed successfully in surgery and shoulder relocated. Damage to Coraco-acromial Ligament, Coraco-clavicular Ligaments and Transverse Humeral Ligament. 47 internal stitches, 25 external.

Stab wounds to lower right abdomen and upper left pectoral. No organ perforation. 98 external stitches to abdomen, 32 external stitches to left pectoral.

Torn intercostals present to right side of ribs. Bruising present from previous injury, no new fractures present. 3 months minimum leave of duties pending successful physiotherapy and psychoanalysis.

Prognosis: One very sore and grumpy soldier. -

You hit the "send" button on your work browser and sent the latest report over to captain Price before slumping back in your desk chair with a heavy sigh. The metallic tang of Königs blood was still stuck in your mouth from the kiss you both shared in the enemy compound.

You glanced over to the sleeping soldier only a few meters away. An oxygen mask hugged Königs face, his messy dark blonde hair stuck to the sweat beading his forehead. You'd been over four hours in surgery with him, painstakingly removing the tactical dagger that had embedded itself into him as well as repairing various other stab wounds and injuries he'd received in his fight to make sure you were safe.

You'd known from the offset that König was a very private man, you'd been told as much from Horangi and the details König had given you about himself we're few and far between. In the months that you'd known him the only thing you were actually sure of was his favourite colour and animal. You leaned forward and rested your head against the table, you needed to find out more about König and the events that lead up to the complete breakdown in his mental stability whilst on the mission.

As capable of a soldier as he was, König was an instrument of war and the team could not and would not tolerate the risk of him hurting his teammates if he snapped again.

Price, Are you free? I need to speak with you.Dove.

You sat up, quickly typed the message and hit send, staring at the computer screen awaiting for a reply. Not two minutes later you received a notification.

Dove,Got Königs medical report through, cheers for that. I'm free if you need to chat, I'll put the kettle on. Price.

You pushed yourself away from the desk and walked over to König, the man was pale and his usually docile face was etched in unconscious pain.

You gently brushed away some of the hair stuck to his cheek and administered another dose of morphine into the IV cannula on his wrist before quietly leaving the infirmary, nervous butterflies dancing in your stomach as you made your way to the captains office.

By the time you'd reached Price's quarters the man already had a piping hot cup of coffee waiting for you, he greeted you with a gentle warmth that you'd not seen from him before...it was refreshing.

"How's he looking?" Price asked, pouring out his own cup of what looked to be tea.

"He's stable, for now anyway." You replied tiredly.

"Mhm, I read through your report, you've all been through a lot. Earned your rest that's for certain..." Price paused briefly to fish the teabag out of his mug with a small spoon before throwing it in the bin with a wet slap, he turned to face you, giving an expectant look.

"So go on then, what did you need to speak to me about?"

"Königs files." You replied simply.

"What about them?" Prices voice was level, his expression unreadable.

You paused for a moment, choosing how you phrased your next words carefully so as not to sound accusatory in any way.

"I...Sir, when I first got transferred here I pulled up the files on every soldier in KorTac and the 141 and I noticed some of the men had missing information. Important information. The majority of which were all under psychiatric evaluation files. Lieutenant Ghost, König, their evaluations were completely blank."

The captain returned to his usual position behind his desk, his eyes fixed on you as he continued to listen to what you had to say.

"At first I figured it was maybe a clerical error, or poor file organisation from the previous medic, so I tried to dig a little deeper...tried to look further back into each soldiers mental evaluations to find something...a nything."

"Ah? And what did you find?" The tone in the captains voice was flat, he already knew exactly what you were going to say.

"Nothing. I found nothing. No reports, no evaluations. Sir, what happened on the mission with König...it-"

"The Vault Protocol." Price cut in, sighing heavily as he pulled a cigar out from the drawer of his desk and clipped it, rolling it absently between his fingers. You clasped are your mug of coffee, enjoying the warmth it provided your fingers as the captain gestured for you to take a seat at the other side of his desk. Price lit the cigar and ran a hand through his hair before giving a tired sigh.

"The VP, Vault Protocol, allows certain special case soldiers to request that specific sections of their files be redacted and effectively vaulted so they remain completely off grid. Any specific section of an operators file can be requested to be vaulted and, so long as certain conditions are met throughout the period of redaction, not even medical personell such as yourself can have clearance to them."

Well shit, that was a lot to take in.

"Sir, if I can ask...What conditions need to be met in order to keep these files vaulted?" You frowned a little, hugging your coffee cup a little tighter towards yourself.

"The condition that they get the jobs they need to do done." Price stated bluntly, leaning back into his chair and scratching at his beard. It was evident that he was conflicted about whether or not to be actually telling you all of this.

"Look, the VP isn't for every soldier. It's a protocol designed specifically for select special case operatives. Soldiers who are still extremely effective and successful on the field but would otherwise be discharged, dishonourably or otherwise, due to their field history, personal history and psychological evaluations..."

Price took a long slake of his tea, studying you intently as he did so.

"Don't get me wrong, this protocol? It's unethical on so many levels that, quite honestly, I can't be arsed to think about it. The VP was designed by myself and Station Chief Laswell to protect the soldiers of 141 and only the 141. Even Shepherd and the rest of the bigwigs don't know about it. But, given how KorTac was force merged with us the same redaction opportunity was offered to them. S'only fair, after all."

"And König requested the vault protocol?" You replied instantly, the pit in your stomach growing as to what exactly the Austrian was trying so desperately to hide. The captain nodded and hummed in affirmation.

"König was the first in KorTac to request the VP, yeah. In fact I've never seen a man more eager to lock away so much of himself."

You stared down at your shoes, your heart hammering in your chest as you tried to process everything you'd been told so far. Eventually you met the captains gaze again, your own expression resolute and steadfast.

"Sir, I need clearance to access Königs files. What happened on the mission...I can't let it happen to him again, I need to be able to help him and I can't do that properly if I don't know the cause for what made him snap. Please, sir. I can't see him like that again and I can't risk the safety of the other soldiers who work with him in the field. If he was responsible for harming one of his own it...it'd crush him, sir."

Price regarded you silently for what felt like forever, despite his usual default calm expression you could tell that the captain was in the middle of an internal battle of weighing up every pro and con to giving or denying you your request. Honestly you didn't blame him, not only was it a huge personal risk to himself but also could prove to be extremely damaging to König if the information wasn't handled in the correct manner.

Eventually the captain leaned forwards, taking one last long drag of his cigar before crushing it into the ashtray by his side.

"I expect you'll receive an email shortly, doctor. You'd do well to make sure it's read in private, is that understood?"

"Yes, sir. Absolutely." You nodded your head a little too quickly. The combined relief and guilty curiosity of finally being able to read everything the military knew about König made your heart rate spike dramatically. With that you rose out of your chair, giving the captain a final nod in thanks before turning on your heel to quickly leave his office, you'd never walked back to the infirmary so quickly in your fucking life.

□ □ MEDIC □ □

You practically sprinted back to the infirmary, barely acknowledging the few soldiers that offered you a passing hello. A large part of you couldn't quite believe that Price had told you so much about such a seemingly confidential protocol and your heart was racing to get back to your office and read through every last detail about König that had been locked away.

You'd entered the infirmary, glad to see that the huge soldier was still sedated and, judging by the expression on his sleeping face, not as in as much pain as he was before you left to see Price. Even seeing König frown made your heart ache, so knowing how much pain the road ahead would hold for him made you feel physically sick.

You briefly rested your hand on top of his own, rubbing the back of it with your thumb before heading over to your desk and logging into your emails. Just as the captain had insinuated, there was a single email sitting in your box. Immediately you clicked it open, the email itself was practically blank, save for a fifteen digit number and an unmarked attachment at the bottom of the page.

The moment you clicked the attachment a separate program opened up entirely and you were prompted to enter a code, you copy pasted the long number that Price had written into the email and instantly you were granted access to Königs files.

All of them.

Instantly you realised that König hadn't just vaulted his psychological analysis files, but the majority of his mission details from his time spent with KorTac and even before when he served with the KSK.

Your eyes scanned over the sheer amount of information you had at your fingertips and a small gasp left your lips as your gaze came to rest on the name at the top of the files.

Kaiser Zigmund

You glanced over to König, taking a moment to match the official name on the files with his face. You'd only ever known this man as König, as everyone else on the base did. Hell, up until today you'd completely forgotten that you'd only ever called him by his military callsign and nothing else.

You smiled inwardly to yourself as you continued to stare at the name, you barely knew any German, but you did know a couple of words. Kaiser as a word and name literally meant emperor, so the fact that his callsign translated to king almost seemed like a bit of a step down in the royal hierarchy.

You began the painstaking process of scrolling through each page, the first few of which were listing various physical injuries sustained from the very beginning of his service to the military. König had a long list. Everything from broken bones to perforated kidneys, written up in a similar manner as the report you'd sent to captain Price not an hour earlier. By the time you'd reached the bottom of the list of physical traumas your own body ached in sympathy.

Next came the psychological evaluations. It was these pages that you were really interested in reading through. In order to help König to deal with the emotions and responses he was having you had to know every single prior note written up for him, whether he wanted you to know or not.

Patient suffers from severe social anxiety which is being medicated via 20mg Propanalol. Prior psychiatric reports showing anxiety stems from childhood abuse in the family home.

Well that explained the reason why König wore his hood the majority of the time, and why he was so withdrawn when you first met him...though it still didn't quite seem to explain the way he behaved on the last mission. You continued to read further into his notes, the ache in your chest deepening the further you read.

Operator Zigmund has been offered intensive psychiatric therapy following diagnoses of severe post traumatic stress disorder after the events of Operation Akuma. Following Operation Akuma Mr.Zigmund has experienced blackouts and violent outbursts towards staff when under extreme physical and mental duress. Compulsory leave to complete full behavioural evaluation has been requested before patient can return to the field.

You leaned back in your chair as you re-read the file, your eyes continuously flicking back to the words "Operation Akuma". It seemed to you that whatever happened to König on that mission was one of the defining factors to the breakdown you witnessed. This rabbit hole just seemed to get deeper and you weren't about to stop now.

You scrolled through pages upon pages of mission logs detailing Königs various exploits throughout his time in the general military and German special forces, eventually coming to a section marked specifically for Operation Akuma. You wasted no time in painstakingly reading through every detail of the mission, a nauseating feeling grew in the pit of your stomach the further you got.

The objective of Operation Akuma was to conduct discreet fieldwork into the claims that a group of Taliban fighters were training war orphans to become child soldiers to be used against invading forces. The Kommando Spezialkräft, of which König was operating with at the time, had been sent to Afghanistan to assist with the SAS in regaining some territory back and we're solely in charge of Operation Akuma whilst on tour there.

From what you read in the file, the mission could not have been a bigger failure. König had been the primary operative on the mission and had lead a small specialised task force to gather information on the child soldiers. Due to a tip off to the Taliban, not only did König bare witness to the horrors of children being used as suicide bombers, but he was also the only man on his task force to not leave the mission in a body bag.

You stared blankly at the file for a while, your empty gaze occasionally flicking between the computer screen and König laid out on the bed nearby. To say you'd been in the military for quite some time, you'd had very few dealings with what one could consider to be a "true horror" of war. Of course treating injured soldiers was always hard and some of the wounds you'd seen you could never get out of your head fully...but the things that König had been through? Just reading about it was fucking haunting...let alone actually having to experience it first hand.

Eventually you closed the folder, making sure to exit out of every program you were signed in on for fear of anyone else reading Königs sensitive information. You pushed yourself away from the desk and quietly walked up to the mountainous soldier in your care. Despite the man being wrapped in copious amounts of bandaging, König was still extremely handsome and you were almost bowled over by the realisation of just how strongly you felt for him and the need to keep him safe.

At this point there was little to do other than continue to monitor the Austrians condition, keep his pain medication topped up and assure he was kept as comfortable as was possible given his situation. One thing was for certain and that was he would be a very grumpy, sore and confused guy when he did wake up.

You idly rubbed your lips, your mind wandering back to how you'd kissed him while out on the mission and the expression he had just after it happened. A carnal warmth blossomed in the pit of your stomach and a small part of you hoped that König wouldn't actually remember that particular event taking place.

Maybe you could play it off as some blood loss induced fever dream? Sure. That could work...right?

Chapter 19. Remembering

Edited 28.08.23 - minor re-writes, changes to spelling and grammar.

What's going on...What happened to me? What...what happened to Dove? Where...am I...

The sounds of various medical machines became steadily clearer in Königs ears, his eyes cracking open as he attempted to take in the surroundings. At first the lighting in the room was almost blinding to him and the soldier almost regretted opening his eyes fully.

König briefly glanced around, trying to make heads or tails of what had actually happened. The Austrians head was a jumbled mess of memories that he wasn't actually sure were real, right now as far as he could remember he had gone on the mission to take out the Russian arms dealer.

The mission had gone completely tits up at some point, König gathered that the moment he looked down at himself and saw several thick layers of bandaging wrapped around his body. His icy grey eyes flicked over his own body as he shivered, becoming increasingly aware of the pain he was in. Every muscle ached, his head throbbed and most noticeable was the ever-growing stabbing sensation tearing through his shoulder and abdomen with each breath.

The increasing speed of his heart rate monitor caught Königs attention. This room was too bright, the machines aiding him were too loud and the feeling of the bandages wrapped around his body didn't agree with him either. König squeezed his eyes shut again, forcing himself into taking a steadying breath against the dangerous level of overstimulation that he was experiencing. If he could move in that moment then the mountainous soldier would have got up and ran out of the room as fast as his legs could humanly carry him.

"König..?"

An all too familiar voice caught Königs ears, instantly easing his growing anxiety. The Soldier turned to face you, his tired and bruised eyes softening the moment they met yours.

"D-Dove?"

Your heart sank hearing how broken König sounded. Despite his usual laid back and relatively soft spoken voice, this time was different, he sounded so weak.You were quick to be by his side, taking one of his huge hands into your own as you rubbed the back of his hand with your thumb.

"How're you feeling, big guy?" You failed to suppress the emotional tremble in your own voice.

Königs tired eyes flicked over your features quickly, even in this state he almost seemed to be trying to drink up every possible detail about your features that he could. It was like he'd missed you, even in his unconscious state. "Y-You're ok...I'm so glad..."

You gave his hand a reassuring squeeze, "Of course I'm ok, I'm more concerned about you. How're you feeling? How...how much do you remember of what happened?"

You felt a lump form in your throat as you asked the question, so much had happened in the last mission; the complete breakdown König had, you abandoning your station by his side to help the other soldiers...the two of you sharing a kiss...

Königs eyes narrowed slightly in thought, his gaze briefly flicking up to the ceiling tiles above his head as he attempted to jog his memory. "I remember...der Kampf- s-sorry, the fight...you left me...ran away."

Your heart sank as you heard how sad König sounded, that was how he remembered it? You running away? Abandoning him? You drew a breath in to speak up when he continued.

"Nein...N-no, you went to...to go help? Roach...I remember, Roach got hit...is he ok?"

You quickly nodded your head, your fingers gripping a little tighter around Königs own hand."That's right, Roach got shot, he's fine, don't worry."

""Sehr gut...I'm glad he is ok..."

The huge soldier closed his eyes, settling back a little into his pillow and breathing out a shallow sigh of relief. You sat in silence for a few minutes, wondering briefly if König had drifted back off to sleep. It was only when his large hand turned in order to wrap his fingers around your own that you realised he was still awake.

"I remember some other things too..."

"Oh?" You leaned forward a little in your chair, your heart rate starting to increase again.

"Ja...I remember being...angry. Worried. I-I could not find you anywhere. I thought something terrible had happened to you..." You moved your fingers away from Königs hand, bringing them to rest gently on his forearm. Even in his weakened state you couldn't help but marvel completely at how strong and stony hard his muscles were under your touch.

"Well don't worry, I'm safe, everyone is safe. You just focus on yourself, you need to focus on getting better. Just you wait and see, you'll be up again before yo-"

"You kissed me."

Königs voice was low, matter of fact, his expression reflected just how sure of his memory that he was. A part of you had hoped the soldier wouldn't remember, or would just think of it as a jumbled fever dream induced by stress and blood loss. In that moment you honestly weren't sure what to do or where to look. You leaned back in your chair, the grip you had on Königs arm faltering slightly as you struggled to figure out what to say. After a few agonisingly long moments you drew in a steadying breath.

"Yeah...yeah I did." Your response was barely above a whisper as you struggled to maintain eye contact with the huge soldier in your care. Your heart fluttered lightly behind your ribs as you watched an unmistakable blush creep up across Königs cheeks, his heart rate monitor betraying his calm face by the way it beeped faster. The solider shot the machine a withering side glare, frustrated that he had been caught out by the medical equipment.

Obviously flustered by the now rapidly beeping heart rate monitor, König opted to change the subject slightly, his icy grey eyes flicking from the machine by his side back to your face. "You said we'd play more snakes and ladders...right?"

Dove couldn't help but chuckle slightly, she gave a quick nod and smiled r eassuringly."Yeah that's right, you were...you kinda disappeared for a while, König...truthfully I wasn't really sure what to say to you to bring you back."

Königs tired eyes narrowed slightly as he ran his uninjured hand through his messy hair and sighed in frustration, "Es tut Mir leid, Dove...I am sorry. So sorry. I do not remember much of what happened during...that...I just remember being angry...so angry and worried that I just..."

König shifted painfully in his bed, trying and failing to find a slightly more comfortable way to lay. Not being able to simply walk away from the situation that was making him anxious was proving difficult to deal with, and he had to take a moment to process what exactly he was saying to stop himself from tripping over his words when speaking to you.

"I remember being in a dark place. A bad place. B-but then I heard your voice. It was...beautiful."

You felt Königs large hand cup the side of your face, his thumb brushing away a tear you didn't even realise was rolling freely down your cheek. You closed your eyes and leaned into his calloused hand, savouring the warmth it brought you.

Now you weren't normally the emotional type. Granted, you weren't like Ghost, who at this point you were convinced was pretty much void of the majority of emotion. No, you weren't like that at all. You weren't emo-tionless, but you were a professional, the whole crux of your job dictated that you kept a level head at all times. After all, you couldn't help injured or dying soldiers if you were a sobbing blubbering wreck.

But this man? He did something to you, to your professionalism, to the emotional wall you'd naturally built up around yourself in order to help you do your job.

Knowing that König was here, sat in front of you, alive, was more relief than your heart and mind could feasibly process. One by one more tears began to roll from your eyes until you felt like you were drowning in them. The moment König became aware of just how much you were crying his glacial eyes widened in a mixture of panic for how to actually help you and general worry that you were ok.

With your head bowed and your eyes squeezed shut in an attempt to stop the onslaught of tears you'd paid little mind to how König had briefly pulled his hand away from you, nor were you aware of the sound of rustling bedsheets while you choked back a sob. It was only when you felt an immensely comforting pressure around your waist pulling you forward that you opened your eyes to see König had managed to sit upright and hang his legs off of the side of the bed to pull you into him for a hug.

For a few moments you froze, your body processing what was happening before the realisation hit you and you sank into the huge soldiers embrace. His skin was warm, a little clammy from the pain and stress in his body but in that moment König could have been a sweating stinky mess and you'd still stay right where you were.

You nuzzled into Königs neck, gently wrapping your own arms back around him, as your eyes briefly flicked down you noticed that Königs right arm, the one that had been badly injured in the mission, was simply hung down limp by his side. Despite you putting it in a sling it seemed that König had been so determined to give you a proper hug that he had managed to pull himself free of the binding, though either from pain or lack of muscle co-ordination due to the sheer level of trauma he couldn't actually complete his embrace with two arms.

You allowed yourself to drink in König's scent a few moments longer before pulling away and gesturing to the bed. "Let's get you back in a more comfy position, alright?"

The mountainous soldier glanced over to his pillows, unable to deny how plush they looked. He said nothing, simply giving you a tired smile and a brief nod before clumsily working his way back on the bed properly. It took a few minutes and a little teamwork but eventually he was back resting properly.

You quickly wiped the last few stray tears away from your eyes and turned away briefly to fiddle with one of the machines by Königs bedside, if anything simply to try get your fucking act together before you spoke to him again. After a moment of giving yourself a stern talking to mentally you turned back to face the injured soldier and pointed to the now empty sling across his chest.

"There should be an arm in that." You teased playfully, a little grin forming as you watched Königs gaze flick down to his chest and then briefly over to his injured arm laying limp beside him.

"Ja...My bad." König gave you a tired smile, his eyes fixated on you as he watched you gently grasp his arm and manoeuvre it back into the sling. You leaned over him, focused in that moment at making sure your patient was in a comfortable position, your movements slowing every time König so much as winced.

Eventually König was back in a more agreeable position and honestly just the act of hugging you seemed to have completely drained him of what little strength he currently had. The hulking soldier regarded you with heavy eyes, evident that he was fighting against slipping back into a deep sleep.

"I'll let you rest, ok? If you need me then I'll be right with you." You half whispered as sat back in your chair, giving your patient a gentle pat on the back of his hand before getting up to go update your reports. It was only after you stood to take your leave that your hand was enveloped in König's much larger one.

You glanced back down to the soldier in your care, even in his weakened state his grip was steadfast and unwavering. König studied you for a moment, seemingly drinking in your features before increasing his grip on your hand, tugging you towards him and locking his lips against your own.

Every ounce of breath in your lungs seemingly vanished in that moment. Your mind struggled to process what was happening, the feeling of his rough stubble grazing your face, his calloused hands entwining in your own...his slick warm tongue dancing in your mouth in ways you'd never thought imaginable.

Eventually, and to your absolute displeasure, König broke away, ending the kiss he had so effortlessly started. His glacial grey eyes bore into your own, a red hue spreading across his pale face as the heart rate monitor once again betrayed just how much his cardio rhythm had increased by. You both shifted your gaze to the machine by the bedside almost simultaneously before facing back to each other and laughing.

Despite the circumstances, in that moment you could've both happily stayed trapped in time within the infirmary endlessly.

-

AUTHORS NOTE

Hello friends! I'm so sorry it's taken so long to publish the next chapter! Life has been very busy of late. I opted for a different style of artwork this time, more anime vibes. There isn't enough anime König at all! I'm actually debating on making a comic based on this story and making a little Patreon for it if that would be something ya'll are interested in! I'm still deciding on an art style for it. Anime style or my usual style seen in previous chapter headers? Hmmm. Let me know!

Chapter 20. A Little TLC

It had been a month since the mission intercepting the arms dealer base, a month since König had narrowly avoided death and a month since captain Price had allowed you access to all of the files and sensitive information that König had kept vaulted.

You'd not mentioned a thing about what you'd learned to König. As far as the colossal soldier was aware he was still as much of a mystery to you as he was with his team mates and you planned to keep it that way unless absolutely necessary. You doubted he would take kindly to the notion of finding out you'd been spying on him.

You been sat at your desk a while, scrolling through the progress reports you'd written up regarding Königs recovery over the past four weeks. All things considered he was doing well, the more minor injuries had healed with relative ease and even the deep abdominal wound was causing little issues other than general discomfort if movement was too sudden. The main issue was with Königs shoulder. The damage caused to the soldiers muscles, ligaments and tendons were proving to be extremely slow in their healing process. His arm was weak, shaky and always in some state of pain, which certainly didn't bode well for his mood. Especially not today it seemed.

König laid on top of the hospital bed, the toned muscles in his chest rising and falling in a steady rhythm as he stared blankly at the tiles on the ceiling. He'd been in the same position for the majority of the morning and had refused to eat any breakfast that you'd brought him.

You pushed yourself away from your desk and walked quietly over to your patient, waiting a few moments to allow him to notice you before waving a hand in front of his face when it became apparent that he wasn't paying attention.

"Hellooo? Earth to König? You good, big guy?"

The soldiers gaze flicked over to you, his previously stony expression softening ever so slightly as he silently studied your features.

"Ready for some lunch?" You asked cheerily. "Nein." "You didn't have any breakfast though." "I know." "You need to eat something, goofball. It'll slow your healing if you don't.""Mhm." Königs icy eyes flicked back towards the ceiling of the infirmary, seemingly now tired of listening to you nag him about the importance of a good diet. You sighed in slight annoyance before turning to fiddle with one of the machines by his bedside.One way or another you were determined to get the man eating and at least in slightly higher spirits.

"Fancy playing a game?" You remained focused on the machine, noting in your peripheral vision how König hadn't so much as twitched at the mentioning of playing a board game with you.

"Nein, danke." König mumbled.

"Not even snakes and ladders?" You feigned shock, putting a hand in front of your mouth. Königs head snapped to your direction, his eyes narrowed in annoyance that you could tell he was trying to keep under control.

"Dove. Please. I am not in the mood for food or games today."

You stood quietly for a little while and weighed up your options. The way you saw it you had three possible routes to choose from:

Option one: Walk off, get on with work and leave König to sulk and hopefully get some rest.Option two: Continue to push König to try eat and no doubt annoy him more than you already were.Option three: Let him have his way with not eating and take a more gentle approach to try get into his headspace a little more.

"Ok, alright, I'm sorry, König. You don't have to eat right now if you don't want and if you're not in the mood for board games that's fine too."

Option three it is.

"You aren't yourself today, König. What's on your mind? Need more painkillers?" Your voice was hushed and gentle as you laid a hand on Königs thigh, giving it a gentle pat as if to spur him into talking.

The mountainous soldier twitched slightly at your gentle touch, his eyes glancing down at your hand before taking a steadying breath.

"How long is this going to take, Dove?" He gestured to his injured arm.

You leaned back in your chair a little and hummed in thought, "Well, it was a bad injury, König...its only been a month. It needs more time."

"How long." It wasn't a question so much as it was a statement. "Three months." You replied quietly. "Three months!?" König sat upright, his expression a mixture of shock and outright anger. "Dove, I cannot be out of action for three months!""Well you are." You stated simply. "What if a mission comes up?" "You wont be going on it.""What if the team need me!?" "They'll have to manage." "But what if-" at this point König was in the middle of a full on ramble, his accent becoming thicker as his panic and stress grew with the thought of being inactive for so long.

Despite the fact that he was behaving like a spoilt child, your heart really did bleed for Königs predicament. The man was an active and extremely useful member of KorTac and, since the merge, the 141 too. You remember Horangi talking to you about his situation, how being grounded on base was more damaging to the Austrian than actually being out on the field injured. But this time was different. You removed your hand from Königs thigh, lifting a finger to his lips in a signal for him to hush. He did as he was told.

"Give me a moment..." your voice was level as you removed your finger from his lips and walked over to one of the drawers by your desk. You took out a small hand gun, nothing fancy, and walked back over to be by your patients side. König eyed you suspiciously, opting to remain silent until you made your point.

You flipped the small pistol in your hand, holding the muzzle and pointing the grip towards König in offering. "Grab it." You stated simply. The soldier instantly lifted his left hand to take the weapon from you, but it was withdrawn from his reach by a few inches before he could grasp it.

"With your other hand."

The soldier lowered his good arm back down and gave the thick bandaging on his right shoulder a dirty look before shakily attempting to remove his injured arm from its sling. He'd manage to free himself and take the pistol from you, but the moment he attempted to hold the weapon out properly as he would on the field he doubled over in pain, dropping the gun with a clatter against the infirmary tiles.

You stood up, wrapping a supportive arm around Königs chest whilst he caught his breath.

"And thats precisely the reason why you're grounded for that long. König your injuries were grievous. Tendons, ligaments, muscles, all of it was damaged. I know how badly you want to get back to work, trust me, and I'll help you get back on your feet as quickly as I can with some intense physio once you've healed just a little more...but right now? How do you expect to be of much use when you cant even hold a pistol, let alone an assault or sniper rifle?"

König stared at you through a curtain of messy dark blonde hair, hurt evident on his features as he processed everything you'd just said to him. He knew it made sense and he knew that you knew that deep down he was inclined to agree...but it didn't stop it from hurting his heart any less.

Eventually the soldier slumped back against the bed, blowing idle strands of hair away from his face before sighing heavily. You thought for a moment he almost looked like he was about to burst into tears.

"How soon before we start physio..." his voice was barely a whisper. You leaned in and rested a hand on Königs forearm, drawing soothing circles and figures of eight on his skin which broke into goosebumps at the tickling feeling.

"Not long, I promise. Give yourself another week, just one more week." You whispered back, your fingers trailing their way up past Königs bicep and onto his chest.

"Th-then we start...?" His voice hitched in his throat as you continued drawing calming circles across his toned pectoral, fluttering eyelids and slower breathing a testament to how relaxed and pliable he was becoming due to your touches.

"Yep, then we start." You gently confirmed, a warm smile playing on your lips as you watched one of the most dangerous soldiers the military had to offer leaning into you, chasing the feeling of your touch.

You leaned a little closer to him, his ear only a few inches from your lips. "Three months might be a lot of time to have off, but don't worry too much..."

Your finger wandered dangerously close to one of Königs nipples before stopping short and trailing back down his arm. The man did well to stifle a mewl, swallowing hard.

"...you'll get plenty of TLC while you recover."

-

AUTHORS NOTE

Yeeeeshh is it getting a little hot in here or is it just me!? The next chapter is gonna be saucy so youve been warned! Id value your input on something though!:

So far I've tried to remain as free with doves appearance and gender as possible so that you can tailor it to your own imagination. So what im debating on doing is writing the saucy chapters with a male and female Dove scenario. (Essentially two separate chapters that are pretty much exactly the same but edited to tailor both genders) they'd be titled something along the lines of "SAUCE - M" and "SAUCE - F" respectively.

What do you reckon? Let me know!

Chapter 21. Rewards (FEMALE READER)

((+18 CHAPTER))

Edited 12.06.23 - cover art added

-

"Come on, big guy. You can do it."

"D-Dove, I-"

"Hang in there, just a little longer."

"I-I can't, I'm gonna-ngh!"

König dropped the dumbbell with a heavy thud, the sound echoing through the gym walls. Just as you promised him, you'd begun intense rounds of physiotherapy after another week of bed rest to try get the soldier back up and in working order as quickly as possible. Despite Königs best efforts it was proving to be exceptionally taxing on both his body and mind.

"Schieße...schieße! Gott verdammt!"

You watched silently as König stormed over to the weight he had dropped, kicking it with as much strength as he could muster across the gymnasium floor, his frustration boiling over into rage. It was the third time this week that he had failed in this particular exercise and what had started as bright optimism to get back in the field was quickly becoming a bone of contention for the two of you.

"Why can I not just move onto a different exercise?"

König stomped back over to you once he had finished with his tantrum. He'd been laid out in the infirmary for so long that seeing his colossal size towering next to you still occasionally came as a surprise.

"You need to be able to do this exercise before we can move onto the next one. Its only going to get harder, König." You rested your hands on your hips before glancing over to the dumbbell that had been launched across the room. "Gonna give it one last try?"

König peered down at you as he held his throbbing shoulder with his free hand. "If I couldn't do it a moment ago then what makes you think I will be able to do it now."

It wasn't a question, more of a frustrated statement.You thought for a moment, staring down at your shoes before you met the enormous soldiers gaze with a sly smirk.

"Because if you do it this time you'll get a reward."

König, who had started making his way back over to the dumbbell, paused in his tracks, turning back around to face you with a raised eyebrow.

"A...a reward?"

"Mhm" you confirmed, your smirk growing as the soldier took an almost cautious step back towards you.

"What kind of reward?" Königs voice deepened slightly, his expression unreadable as he studied you. You took a step towards him, closing the distance between the two of you and offered your most innocent smile.

"You manage to complete that exercise and I'll give you a nice rub down after as a job well done."

Königs crystalline grey eyes widened and a red tinge instantly spread across his cheeks.

"E-excuse me?"

"I said if you get this exercise done I'll give you a nice rub down, you know? A massage?"

You grinned as you quietly observed Königs reaction to your offer. Since you first kissed him out on the mission, the dynamic of yours and Königs relationship had changed somewhat. Due to his injuries you'd naturally spent every day with the hulking soldier, making sure his needs were met and he was kept comfortable...but other than the odd kiss and tease here and there, the romantic progress remained at somewhat of a standstill.

You aimed to change that. You were tired of waiting and god only knows König was far too anxious and polite to make any real moves other than the occasional kiss when he was feeling extra brave or especially high on the pain killers you'd been giving him each night.

You closed the gap between the two of you, gesturing briefly with a nod of your head to the dumbbell, a sultry smirk playing on your lips.

"Well? Gonna do it?"

König didn't give you a reply. The colossal soldier widened his stance slightly and squatted down to grab the dumbbell, giving his injured shoulder a brief rub with his free hand before standing back up to his full height. He allowed the weight to rest freely in his fingers for a few moments, readjusting to the feeling and giving himself time to get over the frustrating voice of doubt trying to worm its way into his head.

You gave a reassuring smile and took a small step back, watching silently as König retried the exercise.Just as you thought, your words of encouragement and the offer of a reward was enough to spur the colossal soldier into finally succeeding in the exercise.

König dropped the weight with a slam, giving little regard to the splintering floor beneath the two of you and turned to face you with a pearly white grin, pride evident on his features.

"Finally! Its about time you stopped dicking around and got the job done." You gave König a playful slap on the back, grinning at the way he rolled his eyes at your remark.

"Pshh! I was simply...testing the limits of your patience." König winked, grimacing slightly as his shoulder twinged in protest of being put to work so strenuously. You laid a gentle hand on your patients bicep, briefly admiring how the muscle felt under your fingertips.

"I reckon you've earned that reward i mentioned. Wouldn't you agree?"

Your voice became a little quieter, more sultry. The change in vocal tone wasn't lost on König, who seemed to only just remember about the reward you'd offered him. He swallowed thickly, his crystalline grey eyes widening at the prospect of you giving him a massage.

"I-I..." a deep breath to steady impure thoughts."Ja-I mean y-yes...yes I have earned my reward."

You closed the gap between the two of you, giggling at how the enormous man in front of you seemed to be struggling to keep composure. You stretched up, snaking your fingers around Königs T-shirt collar and gently tugging him down to meet your face. You leaned into his ear, your lips centimetres from his skin.

"Ok, good. Then go get cleaned up. You smell like a sweaty teenage boy."

König bolted back upright, his expression seemingly unsure of if to be amused, aroused or insulted as he watched you leave the gymnasium.

"I'll be at your room in one hour." You shouted over your shoulder, a smirk playing on your lips as you left the room without giving König a backwards glance.

□ □ MEDIC □ □

Ok...we agreed to this, so here we go...You knocked softly on Königs door. Ignoring the lump beginning to form in your throat. The previous bravado you'd displayed in the gym seemed to be evaporating rapidly as you stood and patiently waited to be let into your patients quarters.

It wasn't long before you heard a distinct shuffling from behind the wood panelling, the metal handle bowing down as König opened the door perhaps a little too enthusiastically. He'd got himself washed and free from the sweat and grime of his physio workout with you and he looked absolutely to die for.

The man was shirtless, a few drops of sweet smelling shower water still clinging to his tanned skin. A small part of you wondered how it was that the man actually had a tan given that his gear kept him almost completely concealed and they were based in one of the coldest places on the planet. His hair was tied up in a messy bun, strands of blonde hair framed his face perfectly.

"Come in." The soldier gestured warmly, shifting to the side of the room wall to allow you to squeeze past his colossal frame. You made your way into the room, immediately perching on the end of Königs bed and smiled to yourself as you drank in the scent around you. This was the first time since you got back from the mission that you'd been in the Austrians room, despite its humble layout and the fact you'd only ever been in there once before it was a welcome change from spending all of your time together in the infirmary.

König rubbed the back of his neck, a few stray beads of shower water running down his skin as he did so. He seemed to regard you for a moment, steel grey eyes meeting with your own before he mustered up the courage to come and join you, sitting on the bed beside you.

"So, how do you think todays session went?" You asked casually, hoping the small talk would put the soldier at ease in the much smaller space. König glanced away for a moment, his eyes narrowing in brief thought before he focused back on you and smiled. "I think...that it went well. Danke, for...for putting up with my lack of patience, Dove." His tone was apologetic as he offered you a slanted smile, evidently a little embarrassed at how he threw a temper tantrum in the gymnasium earlier.

You grinned, shaking your head slightly, "I know its frustrating for you, I really do. It must be difficult being cooped up on base doing a whole lot of nothing when it feels like everyone around you is doing everything-" You paused briefly, laying a reassuring hand on the top of Königs thigh, patting it lightly. "-I'm proud of you, big guy. You've healed amazingly all things considered, and this-" you ran a finger over the fresh scar on his shoulder, "-looks pretty badass. How's it feeling?"

König swallowed at your touch, a small blush spreading across his cheeks at your compliment. He lifted his injured arm, rolling his shoulder slightly to test the waters of its stability and winced. "It is getting stronger, but still hurts." You smiled gently, turning your body to fully face the huge soldier. "Well then it's a good job you earned yourself that reward, isn't it?"

Grey eyes widened as König processed what you'd said to him, the blush he already wore on his cheeks growing deeper."Ja, I-I suppose it is."

You smirked, shuffling yourself further back onto the bed and squirmed your way behind König, the soldiers muscles tensed as you disappeared from his line of sight, seemingly lost behind his broad shoulders. You propped yourself up onto your knees, resting a gentle hand on the side of Königs shoulderblade to acclimate him to your touch. You leaned into him, breath tickling his skin as you gave him his one and only instruction.

"Just close your eyes and relax."

König said nothing, instead opting to draw in a deep, steadying breath before gently exhaling away the last dregs of lingering anxiety.

You got to work immediately, small hands deftly kneading the tight muscles around Königs neck. You smiled inwardly as each knot you managed to work out earned you a relieved sigh from your patient. The feeling of the colossal mans skin under your fingers was akin to electricity coursing through your palms, smooth tanned skin met with the stark contrast of ridged scarring, each one a brutal reminder of the unforgiving and hazardous profession he had.

Once you were happy that the knots had been worked out of his neck, you shuffled to the side to work on loosening up his left shoulder. This side had remained uninjured from the last mission, and you were thankful that the only scars your fingers ran across were older ones. You managed to to get a brief glimpse of Königs face from the angle you were massaging him, grinning at the look of absolute relaxation and enjoyment on his features.

Just as you did before, once you were happy with the condition of his rejuvenated muscles you shimmied to his other side. You couldn't help but feel a pang of sadness as you studied the freshly healed scarring on his right shoulder, the long incision dotted either side by punctures made from the needle you'd used to piece him back together. On a superficial level the wound almost looked completely healed, save for the fresh pink colouration compared to the pale tone the older scars had taken on.

You were extremely careful with how you treated the area, opting to gently rub rather than use more force in your fingertips like you had with Königs other muscle groups. You traced the fresh scar with your finger, earning a slight twitch from König, the area evidently more sensitive to touch, though not necessarily negatively. You spent a good chunk of time running gentle circles across the Austrians battered skin, constantly reading his expressions for hints of discomfort when you dared to apply a little more pressure to the bundle of muscles surrounding his injured shoulder.

For the most part König remain the picture of absolute tranquility. A seemingly involuntary, almost purring sound rumbled lowly from within Königs chest as you managed to gently ease out some of the accumulated tension from the joint."Doing ok?" You whispered so as to not startle. "Mm'mgood~" Königs voice was low, words stuck together as he mumbled a response back to you.

Once you were satisfied that your patient was relaxed you cleared a little space between the two of you, hooking delicate fingers under one of Königs arms and giving him a gentle pull to coax him into laying down from his seated position. The soldier complied, his eyes heavy as they briefly regarded you before he laid back on fully onto the bed.

The moment König laid down you changed your position once again, this time clambering on top of him, a leg straddling either side of his tapered waist. Glacial grey eyes widened at the sudden pressure of you sitting on top of him, his trademark blush instantly burning itself across his cheeks as he stared up at you in what could only be described as adoration. You'd needed this for weeks now. Yearned for it. The shared touches between you, the deep but brief kisses every few days when either you or König were feeling brave enough, it was driving you insane and you could tell by the way the huge soldiers breath shallowed under you that it had been driving him crazy too.

You stayed in position for a few moments, allowing König to adjust to your body weight pinning his hips down before leaning over and locking your lips against his. His tongue forced its way into your mouth almost instantly. A low growl escaped from Königs throat as your fingers found its way to one of his nipples, you pinched and rolled the sensitive bud between your fingers, smiling through your kiss at the feeling of a rapidly growing bulge straining under you.

By the time you broke the kiss König was already breathless, his cheeks flushed and heart hammering so hard in his chest that you could see each beat through his pectoral muscles.

"D-Dove I-"

You placed a single fingertip to his lips, silencing him and offering him a look which simply stated 'shut up and enjoy yourself'.

The feeling of his now solid erection grinding against you through his joggers was enough for your own underwear to dampen to a degree you didn't think possible. You sat up straighter, grinding your clit against the rock hard mass begging to be freed from its constraints. König placed strong calloused hands either side of your hips to lock you in place before moving a single hand up under your T-shirt and kneading your breast in his fingers. The feeling of him tracing circles over the bud of your nipple caused an involuntary mewl to escape your throat as you rocked against him with more vigour.

The feeling of his fingers dancing over your sensitive skin was like being struck by lightning and it took all the strength you had to gently pull Königs hands away from your chest.

"I'm the one rewarding you, remember?" You gave a breathy laugh as you tucked your hair behind your ear and shuffled backwards slightly. Already you were missing the feeling of the soldiers rock hard erection against your pants.

You stared at the tent in Königs sweatpants for a few moments before hooking your fingers under the waistline of his pants and gently pulling them down. Instantly you were greeted by the soldiers throbbing cock, glad to be finally freed from its constraints. You ran a single fingertip over the smooth skin of Königs shaft, an action that caused König to shudder harshly and struggle to suppress a whimper.

Throughout your service in the military you'd come to the realisation that the majority, if not all, soldiers that you'd worked with were touched starved, blood thirsty maniacs. Especially the 141 and KorTac it would seem. König was no different in this aspect, so content with being used as a living weapon of war that very little thought or time was given to consider the other urges he might have had.

Your eyes were fixated on the beautiful face in front of you, captivated by how such a mountainous man was melting into your touch as you slowly pumped his overwhelming length.

The feeling of Königs rock solid cock twitching in your grasp sent electric shivers through your stomach and down into your depths, causing your legs to instinctively squeeze together at the mere thought of him thrusting inside of you.

Another cracked moan from your soldier was all the validation you needed to receive to know that you were doing a good job as you ran a thumb over the tip of the Austrians cock, using the bead of precum that had begun to gather at the top as a means of lubricant to tease your fingertips around his sensitive head. A shiver wracked Königs body as he sank deeper into the pleasure you were providing him, his legs beginning to tremble as you brought him closer and closer to release.

"D-Dove, bitte-" Königs accent was thick, his words sticking together slightly as he struggled to stay afloat in his own mind.

"What? Tell me." Your own voice purred in seduction as you locked eyes with König. You knew what he wanted, you could tell well enough.

A bright red blush had spread across the huge soldiers cheeks, his knuckles white from gripping the sheets of his bedding. König stared at you with heavy eyes, his breath coming out in a shudder as another wave of pleasure from your gentle and steady rhythm threatened to tip him over the edge.

"Bitte...s-so close." He whimpered, attempting a lazy thrust into your hand. You didn't give him the satisfaction and loosened your grip on his length, allowing him no friction to use to his advantage.

"You want to cum?" You whispered, leaning into him slightly. König nodded, his breath leaving him in short gasps.

"You sure?" You leaned in closer, his cock now only a couple of inches away from your lips. Königs glassy eyes widened at the sight of you so close to him, his gaze flicking between your own eyes and your plump lips so dangerously near to his length. The thought of him fucking your mouth was enough to very nearly tip him over.

"P-please...Dove."

It was all the permission you required, without wasting any more time you regained a firm grip on the base of Königs cock. Your lips parted as you took the soldier into your mouth, slick tongue quickly getting to work and enveloping itself around the sensitive head of his dick.

You smiled inwardly as a noise part way between a growl and a whimper ripped it's way out of Königs throat, his fingers tangling themselves into your hair as he begun to lose himself completely. You quickened your pace, taking as much of the soldiers impressive length into your throat as you could handle and you could feel Königs grip tighten in your hair.

"Ngh, D-Dove! Scheiße!"

A final whimpering growl was the last thing you heard before thick hot ropes of Königs cum spilled down your throat. You didn't let a single drop of it go to waste and you eagerly lapped it up as the enormous war machine of a man trembled underneath you with a level of pleasure boarding overstimulation.

Eventually you pulled yourself away, though you'd have been quite happy being glued to Königs cock the rest of your life if you were being honest with yourself. You gave your lips a final lick and briefly smoothed down your hair, which thanks to the huge soldier gripping it looked very much like a birds nest.

For a few moments you simply stared at König, observing him and just generally drinking in his absolute beauty. The soldier looked exhausted, physically spent...and extremely happy.

"You good, big guy?" You gave König a gentle pat on his thigh, a sultry smile playing on your lips.

"More than good, Doctor Dove ." König grinned back at you and gave a chuckle. "I think I would like many more of those rewards." You couldn't help but laugh at his reply, carefully crawling from his lower half to meet König face to face, kissing him briefly but deeply. "Then you'll have to be a good boy and make sure you work hard to earn more rewards like that then, won't you?" You grinned, resting your cheek on Königs chest.

"Also...I think we're kinda past callsign formalities at this point."

"Mmh?" König eyed you lazily from his post-orgasm haze.

"Mmhm." You confirmed.

"Mmkay then what am I calling you from now on?" König half slurred, his thicker accent a current testament to how relaxed he was.

You broke your eye contact with the colossal soldier, opting to draw small circles and figures of eight on the opposite side of Königs chest from where you were laying.

"Out there? Dove. But...but in here when it's just us two?" You paused, looking back up into Königs eyes, the man hadn't broken eye contact with you and was intently observing you.

"Y/N...When it's just the two of us then you can call me Y/N"

Königs smile deepened upon hearing your actual name and you grinned as he repeated it out loud to himself to see how it felt on his tongue. You'd hoped that after hearing your own name he would tell you his, despite him being unaware that you already knew it when you searched through his vaulted files.

He didn't say a word about himself.

"That is a wonderful name, Dove. I-I mean, Y/N. It suits you perfectly."

You smiled through the disappointment of him not sharing his name with you of his own volition, inwardly reminding yourself of just how private of a man König was.

"Thanks, König."

The soldier smiled, giving you a kiss on top of your head before settling back into the pillows and stroking your hair with a free hand.

"You are most welcome, Y/N."

-

Authors Notes:

Aaaaaaaaaaaahhhhhhhh WE FINALLY GOT AT THAT DIQUE. I'm so sorry this has taken so long! I'll be uploading the MALE READER version of this chapter soon! It's literally just going to be the exact same as this chapter but just minor changes for if I've mentioned certain anatomy for Dove You know I don't think I've ever written a properly spicy scene in anything before? I hope it wasn't too bad! Thank you so much for being so patient with me my beautiful people - Moth

Chapter 21. Rewards (MALE READER)

((+18 CHAPTER))

Edited 12.06.23 - cover art added

-

"Come on, big guy. You can do it."

"D-Dove, I-"

"Hang in there, just a little longer."

"I-I can't, I'm gonna-ngh!"

König dropped the dumbbell with a heavy thud, the sound echoing through the gym walls. Just as you promised him, you'd begun intense rounds of physiotherapy after another week of bed rest to try get the soldier back up and in working order as quickly as possible. Despite Königs best efforts it was proving to be exceptionally taxing on both his body and mind.

"Schieße...schieße! Gott verdammt!"

You watched silently as König stormed over to the weight he had dropped, kicking it with as much strength as he could muster across the gymnasium floor, his frustration boiling over into rage. It was the third time this week that he had failed in this particular exercise and what had started as bright optimism to get back in the field was quickly becoming a bone of contention for the two of you.

"Why can I not just move onto a different exercise?"

König stomped back over to you once he had finished with his tantrum. He'd been laid out in the infirmary for so long that seeing his colossal size towering next to you still occasionally came as a surprise.

"You need to be able to do this exercise before we can move onto the next one. Its only going to get harder, König." You rested your hands on your hips before glancing over to the dumbbell that had been launched across the room. "Gonna give it one last try?"

König peered down at you as he held his throbbing shoulder with his free hand. "If I couldn't do it a moment ago then what makes you think I will be able to do it now."

It wasn't a question, more of a frustrated statement.You thought for a moment, staring down at your shoes before you met the enormous soldiers gaze with a sly smirk.

"Because if you do it this time you'll get a reward."

König, who had started making his way back over to the dumbbell, paused in his tracks, turning back around to face you with a raised eyebrow.

"A...a reward?"

"Mhm" you confirmed, your smirk growing as the soldier took an almost cautious step back towards you.

"What kind of reward?" Königs voice deepened slightly, his expression unreadable as he studied you. You took a step towards him, closing the distance between the two of you and offered your most innocent smile.

"You manage to complete that exercise and I'll give you a nice rub down after as a job well done."

Königs crystalline grey eyes widened and a red tinge instantly spread across his cheeks.

"E-excuse me?"

"I said if you get this exercise done I'll give you a nice rub down, you know? A massage?"

You grinned as you quietly observed Königs reaction to your offer. Since you first kissed him out on the mission, the dynamic of yours and Königs relationship had changed somewhat. Due to his injuries you'd naturally spent every day with the hulking soldier, making sure his needs were met and he was kept comfortable...but other than the odd kiss and tease here and there, the romantic progress remained at somewhat of a standstill.

You aimed to change that. You were tired of waiting and god only knows König was far too anxious and polite to make any real moves other than the occasional kiss when he was feeling extra brave or especially high on the pain killers you'd been giving him each night.

You closed the gap between the two of you, gesturing briefly with a nod of your head to the dumbbell, a sultry smirk playing on your lips.

"Well? Gonna do it?"

König didn't give you a reply. The colossal soldier widened his stance slightly and squatted down to grab the dumbbell, giving his injured shoulder a brief rub with his free hand before standing back up to his full height. He allowed the weight to rest freely in his fingers for a few moments, readjusting to the feeling and giving himself time to get over the frustrating voice of doubt trying to worm its way into his head.

You gave a reassuring smile and took a small step back, watching silently as König retried the exercise.Just as you thought, your words of encouragement and the offer of a reward was enough to spur the colossal soldier into finally succeeding in the exercise.

König dropped the weight with a slam, giving little regard to the splintering floor beneath the two of you and turned to face you with a pearly white grin, pride evident on his features.

"Finally! Its about time you stopped dicking around and got the job done." You gave König a playful slap on the back, grinning at the way he rolled his eyes at your remark.

"Pshh! I was simply...testing the limits of your patience." König winked, grimacing slightly as his shoulder twinged in protest of being put to work so strenuously. You laid a gentle hand on your patients bicep, briefly admiring how the muscle felt under your fingertips.

"I reckon you've earned that reward i mentioned. Wouldn't you agree?"

Your voice became a little quieter, more sultry. The change in vocal tone wasn't lost on König, who seemed to only just remember about the reward you'd offered him. He swallowed thickly, his crystalline grey eyes widening at the prospect of you giving him a massage.

"I-I..." a deep breath to steady impure thoughts."Ja-I mean y-yes...yes I have earned my reward."

You closed the gap between the two of you, giggling at how the enormous man in front of you seemed to be struggling to keep composure. You stretched up, snaking your fingers around Königs T-shirt collar and gently tugging him down to meet your face. You leaned into his ear, your lips centimetres from his skin.

"Ok, good. Then go get cleaned up. You smell like a sweaty teenage boy."

König bolted back upright, his expression seemingly unsure of if to be amused, aroused or insulted as he watched you leave the gymnasium.

"I'll be at your room in one hour." You shouted over your shoulder, a smirk playing on your lips as you left the room without giving König a backwards glance.

◻ ◻ MEDIC ◻ ◻

Ok...we agreed to this, so here we go...You knocked softly on Königs door. Ignoring the lump beginning to form in your throat. The previous bravado you'd displayed in the gym seemed to be evaporating rapidly as you stood and patiently waited to be let into your patients quarters.

It wasn't long before you heard a distinct shuffling from behind the wood panelling, the metal handle bowing down as König opened the door perhaps a little too enthusiastically. He'd got himself washed and free from the sweat and grime of his physio workout with you and he looked absolutely to die for.

The man was shirtless, a few drops of sweet smelling shower water still clinging to his tanned skin. A small part of you wondered how it was that the man actually had a tan given that his gear kept him almost completely concealed and they were based in one of the coldest places on the planet. His hair was tied up in a messy bun, strands of blonde hair framed his face perfectly.

"Come in." The soldier gestured warmly, shifting to the side of the room wall to allow you to squeeze past his colossal frame. You made your way into the room, immediately perching on the end of Königs bed and smiled to yourself as you drank in the scent around you. This was the first time since you got back from the mission that you'd been in the Austrians room, despite its humble layout and the fact you'd only ever been in there once before it was a welcome change from spending all of your time together in the infirmary.

König rubbed the back of his neck, a few stray beads of shower water running down his skin as he did so. He seemed to regard you for a moment, steel grey eyes meeting with your own before he mustered up the courage to come and join you, sitting on the bed beside you.

"So, how do you think todays session went?" You asked casually, hoping the small talk would put the soldier at ease in the much smaller space. König glanced away for a moment, his eyes narrowing in brief thought before he focused back on you and smiled. "I think...that it went well. Danke, for...for putting up with my lack of patience, Dove." His tone was apologetic as he offered you a slanted smile, evidently a little embarrassed at how he threw a temper tantrum in the gymnasium earlier.

You grinned, shaking your head slightly, "I know its frustrating for you, I really do. It must be difficult being cooped up on base doing a whole lot of nothing when it feels like everyone around you is doing everything-" You paused briefly, laying a reassuring hand on the top of Königs thigh, patting it lightly. "-I'm proud of you, big guy. You've healed amazingly all things considered, and this-" you ran a finger over the fresh scar on his shoulder, "-looks pretty badass. How's it feeling?"

König swallowed at your touch, a small blush spreading across his cheeks at your compliment. He lifted his injured arm, rolling his shoulder slightly to test the waters of its stability and winced. "It is getting stronger, but still hurts." You smiled gently, turning your body to fully face the huge soldier. "Well then it's a good job you earned yourself that reward, isn't it?"

Grey eyes widened as König processed what you'd said to him, the blush he already wore on his cheeks growing deeper."Ja, I-I suppose it is."

You smirked, shuffling yourself further back onto the bed and squirmed your way behind König, the soldiers muscles tensed as you disappeared from his line of sight, seemingly lost behind his broad shoulders. You propped yourself up onto your knees, resting a gentle hand on the side of Königs shoulderblade to acclimate him to your touch. You leaned into him, breath tickling his skin as you gave him his one and only instruction.

"Just close your eyes and relax."

König said nothing, instead opting to draw in a deep, steadying breath before gently exhaling away the last dregs of lingering anxiety.

You got to work immediately, small hands deftly kneading the tight muscles around Königs neck. You smiled inwardly as each knot you managed to work out earned you a relieved sigh from your patient. The feeling of the colossal mans skin under your fingers was akin to electricity coursing through your palms, smooth tanned skin met with the stark contrast of ridged scarring, each one a brutal reminder of the unforgiving and hazardous profession he had.

Once you were happy that the knots had been worked out of his neck, you shuffled to the side to work on loosening up his left shoulder. This side had remained uninjured from the last mission, and you were thankful that the only scars your fingers ran across were older ones. You managed to to get a brief glimpse of Königs face from the angle you were massaging him, grinning at the look of absolute relaxation and enjoyment on his features.

Just as you did before, once you were happy with the condition of his rejuvenated muscles you shimmied to his other side. You couldn't help but feel a pang of sadness as you studied the freshly healed scarring on his right shoulder, the long incision dotted either side by punctures made from the needle you'd used to piece him back together. On a superficial level the wound almost looked completely healed, save for the fresh pink colouration compared to the pale tone the older scars had taken on.

You were extremely careful with how you treated the area, opting to gently rub rather than use more force in your fingertips like you had with Königs other muscle groups. You traced the fresh scar with your finger, earning a slight twitch from König, the area evidently more sensitive to touch, though not necessarily negatively. You spent a good chunk of time running gentle circles across the Austrians battered skin, constantly reading his expressions for hints of discomfort when you dared to apply a little more pressure to the bundle of muscles surrounding his injured shoulder.

For the most part König remain the picture of absolute tranquility. A seemingly involuntary, almost purring sound rumbled lowly from within Königs chest as you managed to gently ease out some of the accumulated tension from the joint."Doing ok?" You whispered so as to not startle. "Mm'mgood~" Königs voice was low, words stuck together as he mumbled a response back to you.

Once you were satisfied that your patient was relaxed you cleared a little space between the two of you, hooking delicate fingers under one of Königs arms and giving him a gentle pull to coax him into laying down from his seated position. The soldier complied, his eyes heavy as they briefly regarded you before he laid back on fully onto the bed.

The moment König laid down you changed your position once again, this time clambering on top of him, a leg straddling either side of his tapered waist. Glacial grey eyes widened at the sudden pressure of you sitting on top of him, his trademark blush instantly burning itself across his cheeks as he stared up at you in what could only be described as adoration. You'd needed this for weeks now. Yearned for it. The shared touches between you, the deep but brief kisses every few days when either you or König were feeling brave enough, it was driving you insane and you could tell by the way the huge soldiers breath shallowed under you that it had been driving him crazy too.

You stayed in position for a few moments, allowing König to adjust to your body weight pinning his hips down before leaning over and locking your lips against his. His tongue forced its way into your mouth almost instantly. A low growl escaped from Königs throat as your fingers found its way to one of his nipples, you pinched and rolled the sensitive bud between your fingers, smiling through your kiss at the feeling of a rapidly growing bulge straining under you.

By the time you broke the kiss König was already breathless, his cheeks flushed and heart hammering so hard in his chest that you could see each beat through his pectoral muscles.

"D-Dove I-"

You placed a single fingertip to his lips, silencing him and offering him a look which simply stated 'shut up and enjoy yourself'.

The feeling of his now solid erection grinding against you through his joggers was enough for your own boxers to constrict and tighten to a degree you didn't think possible. You sat up straighter, grinding the solid bulge of your own cock against the rock hard mass begging to be freed from its constraints. König placed strong calloused hands either side of your hips to lock you in place before moving a single hand up under your T-shirt and gently caressing your chest with his fingers. The feeling of him tracing circles over the bud of your nipple caused an involuntary mewl to escape your throat as you rocked against him with more vigour.

The feeling of his fingers dancing over your sensitive skin was like being struck by lightning and it took all the strength you had to gently pull Königs hands away from your chest.

"I'm the one rewarding you, remember?" You gave a breathy laugh as you tucked your hair behind your ear and shuffled backwards slightly. Already you were missing the feeling of the soldiers rock hard erection against your own.

You stared at the tent in Königs sweatpants for a few moments before hooking your fingers under the waistline of his pants and gently pulling them down. Instantly you were greeted by the soldiers throbbing cock, glad to be finally freed from its constraints. You ran a single fingertip over the smooth skin of Königs shaft, an action that caused König to shudder harshly and struggle to suppress a whimper.

Throughout your service in the military you'd come to the realisation that the majority, if not all, soldiers that you'd worked with were touched starved, blood thirsty maniacs. Especially the 141 and KorTac it would seem. König was no different in this aspect, so content with being used as a living weapon of war that very little thought or time was given to consider the other urges he might have had.

Your eyes were fixated on the beautiful face in front of you, captivated by how such a mountainous man was melting into your touch as you slowly pumped his overwhelming length.

The feeling of Königs rock solid cock twitching in your grasp sent electric shivers through your stomach and down into your own throbbing erection, causing your legs to instinctively squeeze together at the mere thought of him thrusting inside of your tight little asshole.

Another cracked moan from your soldier was all the validation you needed to receive to know that you were doing a good job as you ran a thumb over the tip of the Austrians cock, using the bead of precum that had begun to gather at the top as a means of lubricant to tease your fingertips around his sensitive head. A shiver wracked Königs body as he sank deeper into the pleasure you were providing him, his legs beginning to tremble as you brought him closer and closer to release.

"D-Dove, bitte-" Königs accent was thick, his words sticking together slightly as he struggled to stay afloat in his own mind.

"What? Tell me." Your own voice purred in seduction as you locked eyes with König. You knew what he wanted, you could tell well enough.

A bright red blush had spread across the huge soldiers cheeks, his knuckles white from gripping the sheets of his bedding. König stared at you with heavy eyes, his breath coming out in a shudder as another wave of pleasure from your gentle and steady rhythm threatened to tip him over the edge.

"Bitte...s-so close." He whimpered, attempting a lazy thrust into your hand. You didn't give him the satisfaction and loosened your grip on his length, allowing him no friction to use to his advantage.

"You want to cum?" You whispered, leaning into him slightly. König nodded, his breath leaving him in short gasps.

"You sure?" You leaned in closer, his cock now only a couple of inches away from your lips. Königs glassy eyes widened at the sight of you so close to him, his gaze flicking between your own eyes and your plump lips so dangerously near to his length. The thought of him fucking your mouth was enough to very nearly tip him over.

"P-please...Dove."

It was all the permission you required, without wasting any more time you regained a firm grip on the base of Königs cock. Your lips parted as you took the soldier into your mouth, slick tongue quickly getting to work and enveloping itself around the sensitive head of his dick.

You smiled inwardly as a noise part way between a growl and a whimper ripped it's way out of Königs throat, his fingers tangling themselves into your hair as he begun to lose himself completely. You quickened your pace, taking as much of the soldiers impressive length into your throat as you could handle and you could feel Königs grip tighten in your hair.

"Ngh, D-Dove! Scheiße!"

A final whimpering growl was the last thing you heard before thick hot ropes of Königs cum spilled down your throat. You didn't let a single drop of it go to waste and you eagerly lapped it up as the enormous war machine of a man trembled underneath you with a level of pleasure boarding overstimulation.

Eventually you pulled yourself away, though you'd have been quite happy being glued to Königs cock the rest of your life if you were being honest with yourself. You gave your lips a final lick and briefly smoothed down your hair, which thanks to the huge soldier gripping it looked very much like a birds nest.

For a few moments you simply stared at König, observing him and just generally drinking in his absolute beauty. The soldier looked exhausted, physically spent...and extremely happy.

"You good, big guy?" You gave König a gentle pat on his thigh, a sultry smile playing on your lips.

"More than good, Doctor Dove ." König grinned back at you and gave a chuckle. "I think I would like many more of those rewards." You couldn't help but laugh at his reply, carefully crawling from his lower half to meet König face to face, kissing him briefly but deeply. "Then you'll have to be a good boy and make sure you work hard to earn more rewards like that then, won't you?" You grinned, resting your cheek on Königs chest.

"Also...I think we're kinda past callsign formalities at this point."

"Mmh?" König eyed you lazily from his post-orgasm haze.

"Mmhm." You confirmed.

"Mmkay then what am I calling you from now on?" König half slurred, his thicker accent a current testament to how relaxed he was.

You broke your eye contact with the colossal soldier, opting to draw small circles and figures of eight on the opposite side of Königs chest from where you were laying.

"Out there? Dove. But...but in here when it's just us two?" You paused, looking back up into Königs eyes, the man hadn't broken eye contact with you and was intently observing you.

"Y/N...When it's just the two of us then you can call me Y/N"

Königs smile deepened upon hearing your actual name and you grinned as he repeated it out loud to himself to see how it felt on his tongue. You'd hoped that after hearing your own name he would tell you his, despite him being unaware that you already knew it when you searched through his vaulted files.

He didn't say a word about himself.

"That is a wonderful name, Dove. I-I mean, Y/N. It suits you perfectly."

You smiled through the disappointment of him not sharing his name with you of his own volition, inwardly reminding yourself of just how private of a man König was.

"Thanks, König."

The soldier smiled, giving you a kiss on top of your head before settling back into the pillows and stroking your hair with a free hand.

"You are most welcome, Y/N."

-

Authors Notes:And that's the male Dove chapter! As I mentioned, it's literally the exact same as the Rewards female chapter, just changes Doves anatomy to fit your own! Thank you so much for being so patient with me my beautiful people - Moth

Chapter 22. Warmer Climates

The months following Königs recovery had gone steady and the two of you had seemed to go from strength to strength. While König still suffered with pain in his shoulder every so often, he'd managed to successfully pass his physiotherapy sessions and had since returned to active duty. It was bitter sweet in a way. You'd gotten so used to having the big lug following you around everywhere you went that when König wasn't on base you genuinely weren't sure what to do with yourself.

On this particular day you'd been going through some paperwork at your desk when the familiar chime of a new email dropping into your inbox caught your attention. You placed the paperwork back in it's relevant folder and opened the new email, curiosity tugging at your mind when you noticed who it was from.

Dove.

Drop by my office when you get a chance. There's a cuppa tea waiting for you if you're free now. If not then it won't go to waste. I will drink it.#TeaIsLife

Price.

You couldn't help but laugh aloud at just how informal Captain Prices emails had become since the first time you met him. Despite his generally gruff exterior and grumpy nature you'd found that he had taken on somewhat of a father figure roll to team 141 and seemingly to KorTac too...whether he wanted to or not. Price wasn't the most emotional man on campus, but these little snippets of humour here and there were just enough to let his crew know that he cared about each and every one of them. That had come to include you too.

Deciding not to pass up the chance for a warm cup of tea, you logged out of your computer and made your way to the captains quarters. König and the other men you usually saw on a day to day basis were out in the field running various training drills, something the Austrian soldier had missed dearly during his recovery period.

By the time you got to the Captains office you noticed the door was already open and peering through you could see Price sat behind his desk flicking through a file. He noticed you almost instantly, the corners of his mouth twitching into a brief but warm smile.

"Knew you wouldn't pass up a cuppa. Shut the door behind you." You returned the smile warmly, quietly closing the door and joining Price at the desk, quickly wrapping cold hands around the still piping hot cup of tea. The two of you enjoyed your beverages silently for a few moments before the Captain begun to rummage in his drawer for a cigar, he eyed you briefly before sliding the file he'd been reading prior to your arrival over to you.

"This 'ere is the intel the lads managed to gather at that compound you and König helped to raid a few months back. Did you read through any of it after it was acquired?"

You paused mid drink, putting your cup back down and linking your fingers together. "No, sir. Truthfully the intel was the last thing on my mind, I had casualties to deal with and it was Lieutenant Ghost and Horangi that found and handled the information they'd found. I've not seen anything to do with it."

Price took a long and steady drag of his cigar, puffing out a satisfying smoke ring towards the ceiling and tapping the table that separated you both idly.

"Thanks to this file here, we've good reason to believe that a man by the name of Vladimir Makarov has ties with arms dealing both here in Russia but also excessively close to United States soil. These papers indicate that a rebel group in Las Almas, Mexico, are potentially harbouring missiles."

Your eyes widened, "Missiles? How would you smuggle entire fucking missiles into a country that is wasn't manufactured in? They're not exactly the smallest things."

"Mhm, you're right." Price nodded, taking another drag from his cigar. "Can't exactly carry em in your hand luggage on the plane can you. Which begs the question of how the fuck Makarov did it. If it even was him."

Your circled the rim of your cup, staring into what little dregs of the tea you had left in the bottom. Confusion was etched into your features."You'll have to forgive me, sir, but im not sure what this has to do with me? I mean, im just a medic."

The Captain smiled gently at you, leaning back into his chair and giving a single sarcastic laugh.

"You're not just a medic, kid. You've become a member of the team, fixed up my men and earned the respect of every single one of them in the process. Now I know you've not been stationed with us all that long, all things taken into consideration...But we've been given the go ahead to pack up operations here and hightail it to Mexico to find out just what the fuck is going on over there. So..."

Price leaned forward across the desk, the orange glow from the embers of his cigar lighting his face.

"I'm asking if you're coming with us."

Your eyes widened, the realisation finally reaching you of what Captain Price was asking.

"You don't follow the same stationing protocol as these lads. You know that. You were transferred here to act as medic to us while we were based here in Russia. Say the word and you can be on a separate flight out of here, another medic will meet us in Las Almas."

König. Soap. Roach. Horangi...hell, even Ghost.You'd grown close in your own way to each and every one of the men stationed at the base. What had started as just another point of station for you had become so much more...and you'd be damned if you were going to let another medic take over.

You stood from your chair, offering an open hand to Price with a deter-mined smile on your face.

"Respectfully, sir, I'm not going anywhere. With you 'till the end."

Price grinned at your response, grabbing your hand firmly and giving it a solid shake, his eyes seemed to twinkle in a renewed excitement of having you with the team for the long haul, as well as the relief of not having to try find another medic in Mexico.

"Well then, best get packing your sunscreen and a good pair of Flipflops, because in seven days we're moving out to warmer climates."

Chapter 23. Welcome to Las Almas

The flight from Russia to Mexico was arduous and much quieter than you'd expected it to be. Many of the men that you'd helped on the Russian base had disbanded and been transferred to other stations, their roles to the 141 and KorTac considered fulfilled.

Now the only soldiers that remained with you from the 141 were Captain Price, Soap. Ghost, Roach and Gaz, a young soldier who you'd very little dealings with on base but always seemed pleasant. The amount of soldiers from KorTac who joined the new mission were even less, being König and Horangi. To say that KorTac frowned upon two of their top operators staying with the 141 was an understatement, both Horangi and König had been promptly discharged from KorTacs service. Thankfully for the two of them, Captain Price was more than eager to adopt them officially into the 141 family as permanent residents.

Many hours and several different time zones later you were finally greeted with the sight of the Las Almas soil under the wheels of your plane. The moment the doors opened felt like as if you'd just opened an oven door, the air was hot, dry and such a stark contrast to the bitter Russian weather that you almost staggered back in shock when the air smothered your lungs.

While you had no doubt in your mind that you'd all get tired of the stifling heat pretty quickly, for now you were in your element and simply enjoying the novelty of not having to wear seven thousand layers of clothing to stave off the chills.

"Steamin' Jesus, it's about bloody time!" Soap clapped a hand on your shoulder and flashed you a warm smile before sauntering down the planes ramp to catch up with Captain Price and Gaz. Roach and Horangi followed soon after, both talking amongst each other.

The last two to step off of the plane and onto Mexican soil were Ghost and König. It wasn't exactly a secret that both König and the Lieutenant were men of colossal proportions, though from spending so much time with the Austrian solider you rarely stopped to consider that Ghost was easily the second tallest in the team. The flight had been uncomfortable for the two men to say the least, the equipment and seating not built to handle such powerhouses on long haul flights. König stood by your side, rolling his sore neck and shoulders as he squinted at the harsh sunlight.

"You good, big guy?" You asked simply, noting that he had put his sniper hood on before exiting the plane. This was unfamiliar territory full of unfamiliar people, right now the security that Königs face covering provided him was a blessing to say the least.

König glanced down at you briefly, his eyes narrowing into what you knew to be a small smile behind his hood. "Ja, just stiff from the flight...I think another one of your massages is due." He winked at you, giving little regard to Ghost, who had unceremoniously barged past him. The Lieutenant was grouchy at the best of times, but throw a long-ass flight into the mix and it made for a hardly ideal work ethic.You opted to follow by Königs example of simply ignoring Ghost for now, of all the people on the team you noticed that he and König had the least interaction outside of missions. Perhaps getting to know the lieutenant better could be a project for you to work on with König if you had the time to spare.

The huge Austrian soldier gave you a brief nod towards the direction of the rest of the team, noticing how the group had bundled together and were looking a little like a lost group of ducks. Even the captain seemed a little confused. You both joined back with the team and broke away from König after he'd been cornered by Roach and Soap, opting to stand rather awkwardly by captain Price.

"Sir? Can I ask what it is we're doing?" You glanced around the empty runway, noting no other aircraft other than the one you all came on. Price regarded you for a moment before checking his watch and grabbing a cigar from his vest pocket.

"Waiting on the slack cunts that were meant to already be waiting for us." The Captain grumbled as he clacked the flint on his lighter in an attempt to turn spark to flame. Evidently he wasn't impressed about having himself nor his boys seemingly stood around in the middle of a dusty old runway waiting on...someone.

Thankfully it seemed that Johns frustration regarding the situation had somewhat spurred the universe into action as your attention was pulled to Roach who eagerly alerted the team to what looked to be a small convoy approaching in the distance.You noticed the boys quieten a little as the cars drew nearer. The Captain hustled his way to the front of his group and you saw that Ghost was now seemingly glued to his proximity, a hand idly resting on one of the pistols strapped to his waist.

Through the haze of the suns reflective rays against the ground you could make out just three cars, hardly a welcome party but at the same time you weren't quite sure what to expect. Eventually the convoy pulled up and an unknown hand gave your group a pleasant and non threatening wave from behind dusty tinted glass as the cars came to a stop. It seemed to be enough to put the group at ease as Captain Price broke away from his group to greet the newcomers, though again you noticed that the Lieutenant stayed stuck by his officers side, refusing to let him greet the strangers without some sort of backup in his immediate vicinity.

Surprisingly only two men got out of the first car together, the drivers in the other remaining cars opting to stay in their vehicles. Like Price and Ghost, the two newcomers had a recognisable 'leader and guard dog' formation with the man in front quickly striding up to your captain and giving him a welcoming handshake. After what seemed to be some run-of-the-mill small talk between the two leaders the captain turned around to address you all.

"Right listen up. This 'ere is Colonel Vargas. Leader of Los Vaqueros, we'll be working with him closely throughout our stay here so ears open to what he's got to say."

You all stood silently, a brief look around had you noticing that every last member of the 141 had their eyes locked onto Captain Price, hanging on his every word. The admiration and respect the team had for the man was really quite astounding. Your train of thought was broken as the new man, Colonel Vargas, stepped forward to seemingly address you all.

"Hola y bienvenido a Las Almas. That is to say, hello and welcome to Las Almas. If you don't speak Spanish don't worry, you will know it fluently by the time you leave." The Colonel gave a grin, his second in command snorting in amusement behind him.

"Like your Capitán has just explained, I am Colonel Alejandro Vargas, leader of Los Vaqueros." Without being told, the man standing behind him stepped forward to stand by his Colonels side. Vargas gestured to him, though his eyes remained fixed on you all. "And this is Sergeant Major

Rodolfo Parra, my second in command." Rodolfo gave your team a polite nod and remained quiet as his leader continued.

"Now that the bullshit formalities are out of the way, you can simply call us Alejandro and Rudy. We will all be working together for some time so little point in being formal, no?" The Colonel grinned and brought a hand up to his face to shield his eyes from the sun glare.

"We will all get to know each other very well over the coming weeks. For now let's settle for getting you all back to my home, you will all want a cold shower and some rest I imagine. Vamos."

After being trapped in what was essentially an airborne metal tube of man-sweat and soldier farts for god knows how many hours it seemed none of the team needed to be told twice, each of the team quickly introduced themselves to Alejandro and Rudy before clambering into one of the two remaining vehicles in the convoy.

Captain Price, Ghost and Soap had already gotten into the first car and were patiently waiting for the two Vaqueros leaders to drive them to base. Leaders drove with leaders, you supposed.

"Dove, chief medical officer." You offered your hand out to Rudy and Alejandro, introducing yourself just as the rest of your team had done prior. Both of the men gave you an enthusiastic handshake. "Rudy. Nice to meet you. You're with medical ah? You'll be a most valuable asset to our team, I look forward to working with you." Compared to the Colonels gravelly voice and thick accent, Rudy seemed much more well spoken and had an underlying gentleness to his tone that you'd not thought a man like him would have.

As if on cue Alejandro grabbed your hand, locking it into a firm grip. "I hear that right? Medical? Good! You won't be low on work in Las Almas. You came at the perfect time, amigo." "Ah?" You smiled, happy to be of service to your new officer. Alejandro nodded in confirmation and grinned, his pearly white teeth glinting in the rays of the sun.

"Si. Last doctor we had got captured by the cartel and sent back to us in a barrel of acid. Hah! Good to have you with us!" A friendly but hard slap on the back from the Colonel sent you very nearly tripping over your feet as you made your way to the last available car in the convoy.

Sent back in a barrel of acid?...looks like I've got my work cut out for me...

-

Authors noteYaaaay Ale and Rudy join the crew! I'm gonna upload some more chapter art to the previous chapters over the next coming weeks so keep an eye out for re-released chapters as they'll have some cute art at the top of them like some of the other chapters do Wonder what shenanigans we're gonna get up to in Las Almas?

Chapter 24. An Odd Group

I t became evident to you on the drive to the Vaqueros base of operations that Las Almas was not kind to those who lived on her soil. Women walked the streets begging, their children malnourished and sleeping in makeshift shelters. Armed men patrolled the roads, the acquisition of their firearms in no way legal, though you noticed that they all seemed to turn away in deference as Alejandro's convoy made its way through the city streets.

"These poor people...why isn't the government doing anything to help them?" You turned your attention from the window to Roach, who was leaned forward in his seat and seemingly interrogating the driver of the car you'd been hustled into. The man, who had briefly introduced himself to you as Carlos, eyed both you and Roach in his rear view mirror before focusing back on the road ahead. "No government here, amigo. Las Almas is lawless."

"You mean there's no government at all?" Roaches voice seemed to raise an octave in concern as he watched the driver shrug. "Si. All gone. Muerto." Carlos shrugged as if it was a normal everyday happening of life, which apparently here in Las Almas it was. "Overthrown and killed by cartel de Las Almas." "Killed by...by the cartel that control this area?" This time you joined in, trying to translate the Vaqueros soldiers somewhat broken English. It earned you a nod in confirmation from Carlos, though he didn't say anything further on the matter.

Eventually the convoy came to a halt in front of a modest looking building which you surmised was the Los Vaqueros base of operations. One by one soldiers riding in the other cars in front began exiting the vehicles and gathered what little hand luggage they'd crammed into the boot of each car. You and Roach hopped out, saying a quick thank you in your best Spanish accent to Carlos for a safe ride over before joining up with the rest of the 141.

König had been in the middle car, crammed in with Horangi and Gaz. You noted idly that, despite the intense heat, König was still wearing his sniper hood, an evident safety precaution to sooth himself against the new soldiers he was now forced to be in contact with. He noticed you hopping out of the car behind him, giving a slight nod in acknowledgment before turning his attention back towards the front where Alejandro and Rudy were now stood.

"This will be your home while you work with us." The colonels gravelly voice seemed to echo around you. "Use what is left of the day to settle in, tomorrow you will be briefed, the day after we get to work. But for now? Rest." On that, Alejandro turned on his heels and left, seemingly giving you and the group some space to get accustomed to the area and to explore the base in your own time.

"Briefed tomorrow and the day after we get to work? They must really be in a hurry to get shit done." You spoke aloud, though it was admittedly to yourself rather than to anyone in particular around you. It didn't stop Horangi from joining in and giving his two cents on the matter however, "Psh I was sure we'd get some time to sunbathe or some shit..." the Korean soldier pouted, receiving a withering sigh and eye roll from König in response.

"Horangi, we aren't here for a holiday..." the Austrians voice was tired, his accent thicker than usual from the lack of talking. You could see a distinct sheen of sweat glittering in the mid afternoon sun from behind Königs hood, evidently he was much better equipped to deal with the cold rather than the blistering Mexican heat."Tch...Yeah I know, but I can dream..." Horangi replied with a roll of his eyes.

▢ ▢ MEDIC ▢ ▢

"So what do you think to our new friends?" Rudy said with an inquisitive tilt of his head, watching Alejandro as he flicked through some files on his desk. The Colonel glanced at his friend and hummed in thought before scratching at the sharp stubble on his chin. "I think they're...certainly a unique group." Alejandro replied with a shrug.

Rudy grinned, standing up and walking over to Vargas' office window. He watched as the 141 group grabbed their bags and began the exploration of the Vaqueros base.

"Unique? Mm, I'd be inclined to agree with you there, hermano." Rudy gave a nod, "Their Lieutenant looks like a skeleton, the Sargent has a mohawk and they've got a giant guy who barely fit in the fucking car."

Alejandro couldn't help but laugh at his best friends description of some of their new acquaintances, standing up to join Rudy by the window and partake in a spot of people watching alongside him.

"They're odd, I'll give you that...but I think they'll be just what we need to help Las Almas get back on the right track..." Vargas mumbled in thought, watching from his elevated position as König and Dove carried their bags into the base and out of sight.

"That big one...he rode in your car, right?"

Rudy nodded and shuddered slightly, "Si. Though he didn't say a word to me...gave me the creeps...what is it with these guys and covering their faces?"

Alejandro grinned, a chuckle resonating in his chest as he slapped a reassuring hand on his best friends shoulder, giving him a slight shake and a playful squeeze, "This change of pace is going to be strange for us all, hermano. For those guys too. Let's allow them tonight to settle in. Tomorrow we brief them, get to know them a little better, learn about their individual strengths and weaknesses. They'll help us rid Las Almas of that cabrón El Sin Nombré..."

"Or they'll die trying." Rudy added with a shrug, earning an eye roll from the Colonel.

"Si, Rudy...or they'll die trying..."

Chapter 25. New Vaqueros

"There's roaches in my bloody room!"

"Probably wanted to welcome you home, Gary."

"Oh shut the fuck up, Soap! They're creepy as hell!"

You couldn't help but laugh as you watched Roach and Soap bickering amongst themselves on the far end of the table in the mess hall.

As Colonel Vargas had instructed, you and the rest of the new and improved 141 had taken the night to settle into the new accommodation and get a good nights rest, though from the sounds of the conversations going on around you it didn't seem like many of the soldiers had actually achieved a solid nights sleep in their new home.

"How did you sleep, Horangi?" You asked with a steady smile, watching the Korean operator as he poked at the yolk of his egg with the end of his knife. "Eh. Wasn't too bad, I suppose." Horangi shrugged, his attention seemingly more focused on playing with his food than anything else, "Though I did have a gecko staring at me half of the night from the corner of the ceiling..."

"Thought this place was meant to be the base for Los Vaqueros. Not Noah's fucking Ark." A gruff voice caught your attention, Lieutenant Ghost slammed his plate of breakfast down rather unceremoniously beside you, the action causing both you and Horangi to flinch a little. This was the first time since working with the 141 that Ghost had actually eaten in the same room as everyone else and sat next to you willingly, though you supposed that in the Vaqueros base Simon didn't have the same privilege of having his own office to eat in.

You cleared your throat slightly and shuffled along the bench to allow for Ghost to sit comfortably beside you, swallowing down your anxiety of having the generally grouchy superior officer eat breakfast with you.

"Did you have trouble sleeping too, sir?" You asked politely, watching out of the corner of your eye as Ghost rolled his iconic skull mask up just above his nose to take a bite out of his toast. He seemed to regard you silently for a moment before shrugging, "Preferred Russia. Colder... and a lot less wildlife."

You couldn't help but snort a little in amusement, shaking your head slightly as you picked at the food on your own plate. "I thought you might like the sun?"

Ghost huffed and turned to face you a little more, his hazel eyes narrowing slightly behind his mask, though thankfully not in his usually standoffish way."Me? Like the sun? Dove, I'm from fucking England. I wouldn't know what the fucking sun was if it ran up to me and kicked me in the bollocks. Rain and cold, that's far more preferable to this sweaty shit." The Lieutenant sighed, rolling his eyes slightly at you as you failed to suppress a laugh in response to his opinions so far on Los Vaqueros base.

You weren't exactly sure if it was the clammy weather, the crappy night sleep or the stress of moving to a new base half the world away, but Lieutenant Ghost was actually pretty amusing when he gave you the time of day. It made for a nice change of pace...especially seeing as he'd never taken the time to get to know you since your transfer to the 141, and that was months ago.

"Where's the sentient tree this morning? Ain't seen him around and he's not exactly hard to miss." Ghost said dryly. You quirked your eyebrow in confusion, "Sir? I don't kno-""Your boyfriend. König." Ghost replied simply, looking unfazed as he watched you choke on your juice before turning quickly to face him."I-oh god, König isn't my boyfriend, sir, w-we're just-I mean...""If you say so." The Lieutenant replied with a shrug and got back to eating his breakfast.

As embarrassing as the conversation was, you had to admit that it did make you think. What actually were you and König? There wasn't any denying that you were both close, as colleagues, friends and...on more physical means. But as far as emotions went...you really didn't know where König's mind was at.

You knew that the Austrian soldier cared about you. You knew that he wanted to protect you, keep you safe and be intimate with you...but how far did this bond you shared actually stretch?

"You sucked his dick. That's gotta count for something."

Your internal monologue had you very nearly throwing your breakfast back up in front of Horangi and the Lieutenant, both of who gave you a questioning look between each other as you quickly excused yourself and left the mess hall.

Invasive thoughts: 1. Dove: 0

▢ ▢ MEDIC ▢ ▢

"Price tells me you're an accomplished sniper?"

"Mhm."

"And that you've completed several high-risk missions?"

"..Mhm."

"Impresionante."

Alejandro leaned back in his chair, tilting his head in intrigue as he studied the soldier in front of him. As a way to get to know the skills and personalities of the 141 team that he and the Vaqueros would be working with, Alejandro had decided to chat to each soldier personally.

"A fun team building exercise." That's what Rudy had referred to it as when he was trying to sell the idea to the colonel. But unfortunately for Alejandro, he'd picked quite possibly the worst soldier in the 141 to start off with.

König sat opposite Alejandro, his leg bouncing restlessly as his steely gaze flickered between the colonel and Rudy, who was leaning against the wall not far from his best friend and leader. König didn't like change, he never liked change. Odd, considering his occupation took him to every conceivable corner of the globe, but it was always something he struggled with.

If there was one thing that life had taught him, it was to be distrustful and cautious of any and all newcomers. Keep everyone at arms length until you know for certain that they won't stab you in the back, literally. This mindset had served König well for years, through childhood right the way up to working for KorTac. The Force-merge with Task Force 141 had scuppered that, forcing him to be around new people outside of his team.

König had absolutely zero intentions of getting to know or trust anyone in the 141 when his team first merged with them. He was happy enough with Horangi. Yet Soap had somehow managed to pester his way into his one-man friend circle, followed by Roach and then Dove not long after that...but their dynamic was an entirely different thing altogether, and honestly König didn't want to think about them right now and risk an awkward boner in front of the leader of Los Vaqueros.

And now here he was again, forced to be around people he didn't know or trust, in a place he'd never been, to do some dog shit mission he quite frankly didn't care about, in a climate that he didn't like.

"Maybe I should become some sort of crazy forest hermit...I could live on berries...actually how many berries would I need to eat? Probably too many...plus knowing my luck some hunter would shoot me thinking I was a Sassy-squatch or whatever they're called..."

"Wouldn't you agree, König?"

"Oh...Scheiße..."

König quickly cleared his throat and rapidly blinked himself back into a sense of focus. He'd been that busy daydreaming that he'd completely missed what Alejandro had just said to him, and the colonel was now staring at him with a hopeful expression on his face.

At this point König had three options: Reply to whatever Ale had said to him with a 'yes'. Reply to whatever Ale had said to him with a 'no'. Or play the good old 'language barrier card' and hope to god that the man repeated himself.

"...König?"

"Ja-uh, yes. Absolutely."

"Fantástico!" Alejandro clapped his hands together loudly, "My men will be most grateful to you, König. You will begin first thing tomorrow, si?"

All König could do was nod his head. He hadn't a fucking clue what he'd just agreed to. But whatever it was both the colonel and his second in command seemed to be pleased by it. He rose to his feet, towering over both Alejandro and Rudy before giving a brief nod and taking his leave.

"Time to find Dove...maybe they can find out for me what exactly it is I'm doing tomorrow..."

If there was one thing König was sure about right now, it was that the daydream of living in the forest as a crazy person was sounding more and more appealing.

-